Saving Grace

Saving Grace

GERALD HAMMOND

First published in Great Britain in 2004 by
Allison & Busby Limited
Bon Marche Centre
241-251 Ferndale Road
Brixton, London SW9 8BJ
http://www.allisonandbusby.com

A catalogue record for this book is available from the British Library

ISBN 0 7490 0609 9

Printed and bound by
Creative Print + Design, Ebbw Vale

Foreword

I have tried to keep the topography in this story correct, only altering the details of buildings and places in the hope of preventing any real person thinking that they can recognise themselves among the characters – which are all totally fictitious.

The only serious tampering with places is at the school. I do not know where this is. It is certainly not Dornoch Academy and I am fairly sure that it is not in Thain.

I am greatly indebted to Wendy for her help with the physiotherapy details.

G.H.

1

Later, she was to realise that, if her car had not refused to start, the rest of her life would have been different. But that, she decided, was par for the course. Your life was steered by a trillion microscopic happenstances among which your own decisions were lost and buried.

The car, she decided, had wet itself, the incontinent beast. It did so from time to time and she had never been able to understand why. It so happened that the agency was diagonally across the broad Edinburgh street from where she had, miraculously, found a parking place within sight of where she had gone to lunch with a former colleague. She had every intention of allowing herself a holiday before embarking on any more work. Her last job had lasted for more than a year and she had been able to live in, all found. There had even been a vacant garage in which to lay up her car. She had no extravagances and her living expenses had been negligible. Her finances were thus in better heart than they had ever been. But while the car aired its plugs, or whatever it did, might be a good time to pay a courtesy call on Mrs Whatever-her-name-was and let her know that Nurse Gillespie would be available for another engagement in not less than three weeks time. Say about the middle of August.

She chose her moment and darted across the busy street, wondering how many poor souls she had nursed back towards some sort of mobility after they had tried the same rash act. The driver of a corporation bus hooted at her without lifting his foot but she made it to the other kerb, giving him a gesture that he could interpret as an apologetic wave or a derisory salute, whichever he preferred.

The staircase, she noticed, had received a fresh coat of paint since her last visit; the pity was that such a hideous colour had been chosen, before being applied with such loving care. The agency door, one floor up, had not even received any such doubtful blessing but she was grateful to be reminded, by the name painted in Roman sans serif script on a wooden strip fixed not quite level on the door, that its proprietrix and manager was a Mrs Gilchrist.

She pushed past the agency door. Suddenly, the age of the building was contradicted. The outer office was bright, streamlined and modern. The receptionist's desk was, as so often, unoccupied. Mrs Gilchrist was sitting at the other desk, which she had always preferred to her own stuffy cubbyhole, opening mail. She rarely managed to keep staff for long, but this mattered very little. She was a rapid and accurate typist who seldom if ever took a holiday. The two computer screens were blank but Mrs Gilchrist's memory was phenomenal, as she immediately demonstrated.

'Well, well,' she said. 'Grace Gillespie. How are you getting on with Mrs Swithin?'

Grace seated her tall frame in the visitor's chair. 'Mrs Swithin died,' she said simply.

Mrs Gilchrist pursed her lips. She was a round, silver-haired woman whose enormous heart was nearly always at variance with her keen business sense. 'I'm sorry about that,' she said. 'But perhaps it was a blessed release. Osteoporosis, wasn't it?'

'And almost everything else.'

'Then it was definitely a mercy.' She fixed Grace with the eyes of a spaniel. 'And I have the very job for you. It just came in. Nursing *and* physiotherapy, but not an excessive amount of each. You were a nurse before you took up physio, right?'

'That's true,' Grace said. 'But I only looked in to say that I'd be available in about a month's time. I'm long overdue for a break.'

Mrs Gilchrist's expressive face registered disappointment. 'That's a pity. They need somebody straight away. I'll have to give it to Wendy Morrison – you know her don't you? – but she's really a city girl and her present employer's not quite ready to do without her. This job is away up north of Inverness. You come from up that way, don't you?'

'My parents are in Dornoch. I was born near there.'

'This can't be far away. It's somewhere on the Dornoch Firth, and I gather it's definitely rural. They need somebody straight away, but I wouldn't expect it to last for more than a few months and you could have a lovely long holiday in the autumn.'

Grace knew that Mrs Gilchrist had made up her mind and that it was her technique to keep up gentle, constant pressure, like a starfish opening a mussel, until she got her way. Grace was tempted to resist if only to see how long she could spin it out. But her interest was aroused. It would be great to be back in her home territory, where consciousness of family ties meant that she could trace her relationship to almost any eastern Highlander. And it would mean an escape from the myriad British tongues, some pleasant but some infinitely irritating. Mrs Gilchrist had the prissy Edinburgh accent at its worst, although she would certainly have been mortified to be told so. In the far north and west, Gaelic had been the universal language until quite recent generations and when English arrived it had come in a pure form, with no dialect and, for an accent, only a lilt so soft that Grace was quite unaware of it in her own voice.

She was interested enough to look immediately for the snags which experience had taught her could hide behind the most attractive jobs. 'I wouldn't have to cook, would I?' she asked. She was a good cook and enjoyed the act, but some employers regarded the nurse additionally as a home help.

'There's another man, a retired uncle, I believe, who does all the chores. You might be expected to help out whenever he wanted time off, but he could take over when it was your turn for a break. In general, you'd be looking after a younger man who had a fall from a height and took it mostly on his knees and elbows. He's got some mobility back, but very little.'

'It sounds as if he should really have stayed in hospital. Can they really afford a resident nurse and physio?' Grace had occasionally met up with clients who had run out of compensation but felt that she should continue working just for her keep and the love of her calling.

'No problem there,' Mrs Gilehrist said. 'There's some doubt about who was responsible for the accident, but he has BUPA. Raigmore Hospital has had to close wards because of a superbug outbreak and at least he had the uncle to look after him. The parties got together and decided to fund the post between them, pending an agreement or possibly a lawsuit. He went home yesterday. You'd be paid directly by BUPA.'

Grace thought it over, but only for a very few seconds. The chances of finding another post so close to home were remote and she was quite strong-minded enough to deal with any snags that might arise in a household which, apart from her, would be wholly masculine.

'You'd better give me what you have,' she said. 'Where do I get the case-notes?'

Next morning, Grace said a polite goodbye and thank you to George Tullos, the friend with whom she had stayed the past few nights. George was a lawyer and had a reputation for ferocity on his clients' behalves. Grace and George had been friends since their schooldays. They had also, on occasions, been lovers, but as a lover George had not been quite the tiger that he was in his work; indeed, looking back, Grace found that she had been so unimpressed that she had only a very vague notion of how often they had shared a bed. Half a dozen times? Twenty? More? The act had been more a gesture of friendship combined with mild physical need than an outflow of passion.

Her car was old but well kept and there was no recurrence of plug wetting. She turned its nose to the north. The Forth Bridge was soon past and she was on the motorway. There was sunshine but the car was not too hot with the windows open. The sun was behind her and no trouble except when it reflected off the rear window of a car in front. It was a good day to be alive and driving, going towards a new challenge and yet nearer to home.

Before Perth, the M90 divided. She went left, bypassed Perth altogether, and joined the A9. The hills grew into mountains. Traffic to Inverness had long before outgrown the road, but Grace was content to follow slower traffic until one of the sections of dual carriageway let her pass. If she saw a tailback developing behind her, she speeded up as much as the law and the prevailing conditions would allow until she could let it go by. Her estate car was large and capable of sustained high speeds but it was heavily laden. She kept it and tolerated its thirst for fuel for the sake of its carrying capacity. She was not a fast driver but she was considerate and careful.

She knew better than to venture into the Inverness traffic. She passed it by and soared on the new bridge over the Beauly Firth, turning back almost on her tracks to descend to North Kessock for a late lunch and a chance to stretch her legs along the waterside, looking across the water to the hills west of Inverness. Back on the road she found the traffic less heavy, but this was offset by difficult overtaking conditions so that tailbacks formed behind any vehicles slower than hers. Some drivers snatched at half-chances and bullied their way past in the teeth of approaching traffic, sending Grace's heart into her mouth, but she suffered patiently as far as the long bridge over the Cromarty Firth, where the breeze was whipping up whitecaps to sparkle in the sunlight. The heavy lorry in front of her turned off towards Dingwall, but a few miles further on Grace left the main road, cutting off a long detour and taking a short cut over the hills.

Her road climbed out of lush farmland into hills dressed with conifer plantations or with heather beginning to blush autumn purple. After a long saddle, she gained glimpses of the meandering stretch of Dornoch Firth. It was a view of contrasts – the expanse of tidal water, fringed by agricultural land, pastoral to the point of cosiness with fields and woodland, and all backed by the omnipresent hills.

The road swung over a deep gulley and then wandered down, between conifers and then silver birches, until it came out on another road that twisted along the southern shoreline. She found the house she was looking for, one of a small cluster of three houses, neither old nor new, beside the road and separated from the Firth by a spread of lime-green fields. The name, Strathmore, was incised into a slab of hardwood and picked out in gold, a far more elaborate nameplate than was usual in the area. The garden was tidy and bright with flowers but strictly formal. Whatever could be squared was squared. Even the Virginia creeper on the wall had been clipped off at the level of the window heads.

She pulled off into a short driveway leading to a hammerhead beside a two-car garage and sat for a minute, savouring the quiet, unbroken except for the small clicking sounds from underneath as the car began to cool. Between the houses she could see across the Firth to the village of Spinningdale and beyond it the mass of Beinn Donuill. She could almost make out the house in which she had lived until she was six.

Her reverie was interrupted when the front door opened and an elderly man appeared, blinking in the sunlight. Judging by the height of the doorway, he was tall although slightly stooping. His hair was silver but only slightly thinned. There was little if any spare flesh on his bones.

She stood up out of the car – rather stiffly, because it had been a long drive. As she approached the door, she saw the man's face in more detail. It was a long face, tanned and lined as though he had spent most of his life in the open air. His eyes were blue. She thought that they were narrowed against the sun but she later found that that was their customary aspect. His nose was straight with slightly flared nostrils; his mouth was pinched and he had a prominent chin. Grace thought that the upturned ends of his eyebrows together with rebellious tufts of hair over his temples would have given him a diabolic look until his hair had lost its colour. Now the overall effect was uncompromising but peevish.

'You'll be the nurse, no doubt,' he said. 'Miss Gillespie, is it?'

'Correct,' she said. She put out her hand and after a moment's hesitation he shook it. His clasp was firm and dry but it failed to communicate more than a token greeting.

'You'll take a cup of tea,' he said. It was hardly a question.

'Happily.'

'Wipe your feet. Kitchen's the first door on the left. Your room's opposite. Bathroom at the end of the hall. Put your car by the big rose-bush and it will be in nobody's way.'

He turned away and disappeared into the kitchen. Grace guessed that she was to bring in her luggage while he made tea. She raised one eyebrow. She travelled with a quantity of equipment as well as nearly all her personal possessions. It would have been customary for him to offer to help with her bags, but she had often had to manage for herself. She moved her car as directed and lifted out the first two cases.

Her room was small but it had been brightly decorated in reasonably tasteful colours and in the not too distant past; and at least there were plenty of cupboards showing signs of having recently been emptied. The room did not have the view of the Firth, but on the other hand it looked out on a group of silver birches, Grace's favourite tree. There was even a wash basin tucked into a corner. The wallpaper was an attractive pattern of grey lines that seemed to wander randomly over a very pale blue background with occasional shapes of darker grey. Only later did she recognise the lines as overlapping outlines of female forms and the darker shapes as representing stocking-tops.

It took five more journeys to bring the rest of her luggage, by which time she was sure that her arms dangled to her knees. But at least she had accumulated, over the years, a sufficiency of stout suitcases with strong handles. Thus there was no need of the ultimate enemy of anyone with delicate fingers – cardboard cartons tied with string. She left her luggage stacked at the foot of the bed for later disposal and washed her hands. She could almost have thought that she had the quiet house to herself, but the quiet made a welcome change from having one or more anxious relatives trying to settle her in and at the same time introduce her to the patient and obtain reassurance about the symptoms and prognosis, all this while children rampaged around their feet. She emerged again into the hallway.

Experience had taught her not to be too self-effacing except in times of crisis. Taking the man's parting words to be an invitation, she gave a quick rap on the kitchen door, opened it and walked in. The kitchen was large enough to accommodate a central table that had probably doubled for family dining. The first thing to strike her was that there was no smell of cooking although the afternoon was almost gone. But there was a large teapot under a colourful woollen cosy on the table beside a plate of biscuits.

The man was seated at the table and already pouring black-looking tea into a blue and white china mug. He produced a grimace which was obviously intended for a smile of welcome. 'Come in,' he said. 'Sit you down. You take milk?' His tone was ungracious but his gentle

17

lilt, with a slight accent on the sibilants, made her feel at home. 'I am Duncan Cameron.'

'Grace Gillespie.' She wondered whether to shake hands again, but he bowed slightly and she replied in kind. 'I take milk,' she said. 'But I'm out of practice at taking my tea quite so black.' She added hot water from the kettle, seated herself in a plain bentwood chair and added milk to her mug. 'The patient is not a Cameron too?' she asked. 'I think that the case-notes said Campbell.' She found that her own voice was reverting towards the Highland cadence of her youth.

'Stuart Campbell. He is the son of my late sister. You will meet him shortly but there is no need for haste. He is comfortable for the moment. I have been looking after him for two days, since he came home. I have tried to help him to exercise his limbs but I was afraid that I might do more harm than good. He can do little for himself but at least he can move around in the bed, so there is nó danger of bedsores.' He saw her ever mobile eyebrow go up despite herself. 'I nursed my own father for a year before he died. When you have met the boy, perhaps you will speak to me. I am... concerned.'

'Medically?'

'No. I am sure that he has had the best medical treatment. Given time, I think he will get about again. My worries are different. You have experience of accident cases?'

The question was not intended to be insulting but arose from a very genuine concern, so she contented herself with saying, 'Yes.'

'That is good. But I am not going to tell you what to think. Take time. When you have met him and had time to consider, then tell me if you have any doubts.'

He turned his attention to making his choice from

the plate of assorted biscuits, seemingly feeling that he had said all that was necessary on the subject for the moment.

2

Stuart Campbell, Grace's patient, occupied what must have been intended as the master bedroom, with a broad view across the Firth to the mountains beyond. To alleviate the inevitable boredom by giving the patient a view of the outside world, the furniture had been turned round. Two wall-lights, obviously intended to be over the bed-head, were left in futile isolation on a side wall and the double bed backed almost against a pair of built-in wardrobes but had been kept two feet clear so that the wardrobe doors could be reached. Grace approved. She preferred to have access all round the patient. A television sat blindly by the window, but beside the bed was a light trolley holding an assortment of books and odds and ends, with a radio, tuned to Classic FM, relaying, very softly, Field's Nocturne No 5 in B flat. A laptop computer had been relegated to the top of a chest of drawers and gathered a faint layer of dust. The décor was bright but unimaginative and the furniture was a mixture of the old and new, but all of good quality.

The occupant of the bed was well propped up with pillows, to make the most of the view over a well kept garden just as regimented as the other at the front, some rough pasture where a few Highland cattle were grazing and a panorama across the Firth. As they came in, he rolled half onto his side and, with some difficulty, put out a hand and turned down the music. The bed was tidy and looked fresh. His uncle might be a gloomy old grouch but she gave him full marks for amateur nursing.

'This is my nephew Stuart,' said the older man. He

tried to retain his usual gruff manner but a wealth of affection stole through.

'I'm Grace Gillespie.'

'What do they call you?' He was another in the lean, dark style of many Highlanders. The resemblance to his uncle was unmistakable, but the features combined to create an expression of mild intelligence and humour that Grace found attractive. He was, she decided, a very good-looking young man and, to add to his charm, apparently quite unaware of it. Although his face was pale from his hospitalisation and engraved with lines of pain he managed to produce a friendly smile. He was cleanly shaved except for a neat tuft of beard. Full marks to the uncle again.

'Nurse Gillespie. Or Grace.' She was ready to quell any forwardness on his part, but when he let the subject drop she went on, 'I think we should discuss your case.' She looked at Duncan Cameron.

He took the hint. 'I'll leave you to it,' he said. 'Tea in forty minutes.' Grace knew that 'tea' was probably a reference to the evening meal. The short time-scale suggested that the meal would probably be cold meat and salad. She gave a mental shrug. She could accommodate herself to the whims of her clients, short of vegetarianism. She had never felt able to accept that a diet lacking the nutrients gathered by the more efficient herbivores was sufficient; nor that excluding them from her diet would have been doing the herbivores any favours. Without the patronage of omnivores like herself, they would never have existed at all. But there would be time enough to worry if the culinary tradition of the house turned out to be altogether too austere.

She pulled a heavy, ornate Victorian chair up to the bed and sat down. The patient looked surprisingly undamaged but she knew that under the cotton pyjamas would be dressings galore. Beside the radio she placed her notebook. This was the stage at which, inevitably, she would need a 'shopping list'.

Field's Nocturne was nearing its closing bars. She waited until the music finished. He reached out again and switched off the radio. 'Your uncle has been looking after you for the last few days?' she said.

'He's been doing his best, and a very good best too. He is not exactly a skilled nurse but he is good-hearted. This was his room but he moved me in here so that I could have the space and the outlook.'

Grace had no intention of discussing the merits of Duncan Cameron. 'He says that you can manage to move around in the bed, which lightens the nursing load a lot. Suppose you tell me exactly what happened to you.'

His face clouded. He opened his mouth several times without speaking. 'I don't know exactly what happened to me,' he said at last. 'I took a fall from a roof. I'm told that I must have landed on my knees and elbows but I also gave my head a knock so that I don't remember anything about it. They managed to patch up one of my knees in Raigmore but they had to give me an artificial one on the right. My elbows were a real mess. I still don't have much movement in them and my hands don't work properly.'

'That's for me to work on, with your co-operation. Are your hips and shoulders all right?'

'They're OK.'

Grace frowned. 'I haven't seen your case-notes yet,' she said, 'but the agency had some details. There was some bruising to your spinal cord. I gather that you also managed to bang the back of your head?'

'Yes. It's all right now except for not being able to remember the fall.'

'The knock on the head probably explains some loss of memory. How much time is missing?'

'From being on the roof to waking up in the ambulance. Not long.'

'I wouldn't worry about it. You certainly shouldn't struggle to remember. Either it'll come back or it won't. If it doesn't, it may be because whatever it is is better forgotten.' She glanced at her plain digital wristwatch and decided that she had time in hand. 'Now let me have a look at you.'

He showed the usual signs of mild embarrassment as she replaced the carefully but inexpertly applied dressings. She had rolled him over and was examining his back when his uncle knocked on the door and called to say that the meal was ready. As she helped the younger man back into his pyjamas she said, 'I take it that you can't feed yourself?'

'Only with difficulty. Even if I could get my hand as far as my mouth, which I can't quite, I still don't have much feeling or movement in my fingers.'

He was beginning to show signs of self-pity which, while not unexpected, was to be discouraged. 'I'll come back and help you eat shortly,' she said briskly. 'Are you comfortable?'

He admitted that he was. 'But I don't feel very fragrant,' he said. 'I suppose you couldn't get me as far as the bathroom, between you? Duncan couldn't manage it on his own.'

'Sponge-bath later,' she told him.

* * *

In the kitchen, there was a sumptuous smell. The central table had been laid with a white cloth and Duncan Cameron was putting out two plates of what seemed to be lamb casserole. Another plate was visible through the window of the electric oven. But there was no sign of a pressure cooker or even of a casserole dish. The meals seemed to be a little heavy on vegetables and light on meat. This awakened a memory and she realised that these were pre-cooked and frozen meals. She was relieved. It might not be *haute cuisine* but at least she would not be forced to take over the cooking as an alternative to being exposed to the worst rigors of bachelor catering.

He pulled out her chair for her – a self-conscious gesture that seemed to require an effort of will – and poured tea. She noticed that he added boiling water to her cup. So she was to be treated as a favoured if not a very welcome guest.

'What did you think?' he asked suddenly.

'In what respect?'

He put down his fork and looked at her speculatively. 'You said you had experience of accidental injuries,' he said.

'I did three years in the Accident and Emergency Unit at St Thomas's,' she told him.

'Then you'll have seen other injuries just like his?' He waited, watching her.

'You'll have to be more specific.'

'I will not tell you what to say.'

'I should hope not. All right, I'll say it for you. You want to know whether your nephew's injuries are consistent with an accidental fall off a roof and a landing on his knees and elbows. Yes?'

He said nothing but picked up his fork again, nodding slowly.

Grace suddenly felt that she might be walking on thin ice. An incautious answer might land her in the witness box, testifying in a civil lawsuit. 'That's not really a proper question to put to me,' she said quickly. 'If I give you an answer at all, it's on the understanding that you don't quote me; and if I'm asked I'll deny that I ever said it.'

'That is understood.' From the faintest suggestion of a grimace, she gathered that he did indeed understand.

'Very well, then.' She used the act of eating the last of her lamb as an excuse to delay speaking again. She knew only too well how easily a careless remark could return to haunt the speaker. When her silence had gone on long enough, she said, 'The most I'm prepared to tell you is that I find it hard to envisage how a man could fall off a roof, land on his knees and elbows and manage to hit the back of his head. There were still signs of bruising to his back. There was some mention of earlier paralysis from the bruising to his spinal cord which make me wonder a little. But, of course, I don't know what he may have bounced off on the way down.' There had been other reasons for disquiet but she decided that she might have put quite enough cats among the pigeons.

The subject was allowed to drop. When Mr Cameron realised that Grace had been a local girl, she was immediately dragged into the customary exploration of not only her own family tree but also that of every common acquaintance who they could discover. The information was extracted without comment but she could see that he was not particularly impressed. The meal, as she had suspected, turned out to be 'high tea' and the main course was followed by wholemeal bread with jam or honey and a date-and-walnut cake, all obviously supermarket wares but perfectly healthy and acceptable. When she had eaten her fill the inquisition was still in full cry, but she excused herself in order to attend to the nephew.

The radio was relaying music again but they left it performing softly. The process of feeding the patient was a potentially messy one but careful observation of his attempts to help himself gave her a much better measure of the damage to his joints and nerves. She took the tray back to the kitchen and returned. There was a bowl and a washcloth beside a wash basin. She had brought her own soaps and powders. Her usual routine would have been to provide him with soaps, cloths and water and then to leave him to manage for himself, but his stiff elbows and the lack of manual strength made this unsatisfactory and instead she began the long-practised routine of giving the patient a bed-bath. She was quite accustomed to seeing a man's naked body, but his was above average, almost handsome, although the muscles were losing condition from disuse. The male genitals she had always considered faintly ridiculous, added by nature or the creator in a lewd and whimsical moment. She tried to keep the act of washing as impersonal as she could, but inevitably he began to stir. For the first time she detected a sort of sculptural beauty in the strange addenda.

To relieve his embarrassment she said, 'Tell me what you do know about your accident.'

Gratefully, he accepted the subject as a distraction while she towelled and powdered and got him into clean pyjamas. 'They're expanding the High School where I teach. I'm the depute principal. It's to become a community college serving quite a big catchment area. The older part of the building is on four floors but the extension is on six.

'The concrete frame and floors were in, though mostly bare, so there was the usual topping-out ceremony, with the chairman of the education committee putting in the last spadeful of concrete. There will be several more big contracts in the Region, so the contractor decided to make a real show of the topping-out, with everybody invited and drinks and snacks laid on. I was asked to go along as depute head and because I'd been on the project committee. There was quite a crowd there, what with councillors, school and council staff, the contractor's senior men and representatives from the various subcontractors.'

'Not many people resent a free drink and an hour or two off work,' Grace commented.

He produced a smile that turned his face from modestly good-looking into definitely charming. 'Very true. Also, adding to the throng, the contractor had asked for a few senior pupils to hand round the drinks and canapés. There was a choice of whisky or sherry, I remember, and a selection of soft drinks.

'In the middle of the flat roof there's a square penthouse where the lift machinery and ventilation plant will go. The tables had been set up to one side of that, on the side away from the prevailing wind for the sake of shelter, which was just as well because there was a bit of a breeze. And in the middle of the other side of the roof the contractor had installed a Portaloo, which he'd lifted up by crane.

'The chief executive of the company said his piece and then the Education Committee chairman gave what was really a camouflaged electoral address. After that the company was free to mingle and chat. I made my number with the chairman and spoke to one or two other people, but it wasn't a crowd that I was really comfortable in. I had some work waiting for me, so I headed for the stairs. That's the last I remember.'

The subject was abandoned while she began to exercise his stiff limbs. Every step was made more protracted by the fact that each joint had suffered different damage and had made a different degree of progress. She identified a few exercises that he could manage for himself and warned him not to overdo any of them. Then she took a seat beside the bed.

'Go on,' she said. 'Where were the stairs? I want to know all about it.'

'The stairs run round the lift-shaft and service core. The head of the stairs was in the penthouse and facing the Portaloo.' His manner became evasive for the first time. She was undecided whether to attribute it to loss of memory or delicacy. 'I decided that I wanted a pee,' he said defiantly. 'And that really is all that I remember.'

'What do you think happened?'

'I suppose I went to look down and got too near to the edge. Maybe a gust caught me. I fell two floors. They found me on the flat roof of the earlier building – if I'd missed that, I'd surely have been killed.'

'There must have been a handrail?'

'There was a rope going through posts. That was thought to be enough because the scaffolding was still in place round most of the building. Not above the older building, though, where it had been taken away to allow repairs to the roofing.'

'But –'

'It's no good asking me questions,' he said abruptly. 'I don't know any more.'

29

Grace decided to let it drop – for the moment. The morale of the patient was all-important. She stayed and watched a wildlife documentary with him, but when the voiceover uttered the third or fourth cliché he fumbled with the remote control and killed the sound. '"On a daily basis,"' he quoted. 'Why can't they just say "daily"? They surely aren't paid by the word.'

'It's almost as bad as "At this moment in time,"' she agreed.

Creases appeared around his eyes as he smiled. 'Either we have the same foibles,' he said, 'or you've made a very good guess at mine. If you're going to use the language, you may as well use it with precision. How do you feel about a three-point turn?'

Grace laughed with him. 'Yes. I've noticed that one too. When you think about it, you could only do a three-point turn if you were going to drive away in reverse. Were you always a schoolmaster?'

He looked at her and she knew that he was seeing her for the first time as an individual rather than as a figure from the world of medicine. 'You think I'm a pedant. I'm not really. I did three years in the RAF, looking after computers. That teaches you precision. I tried for pilot training but I could never make a satisfactory landing. My judgement of heights was faulty.' He sighed and then chuckled. 'They say that a good landing is one that you walk away from and it's a very good landing if the plane can fly again. I never could be sure of doing either of those, but I never made as bad a landing as I did on that roof.'

'I heard that it's a good landing if you can open the doors of the plane afterwards,' she said.

Suddenly he gave a deep belly laugh. Their eyes met

and she knew that they would get along. She settled him for the night and then went to unpack and bestow her belongings.

3

The bed was unfamiliar but comfortable and Grace Gillespie slept deeply. She woke, later than her usual, to small sounds in the house.

She showered and dressed in her personal version of a professional uniform, a pale grey polyester and cotton dress so crisply clean that the observer might have expected her to crackle. She looked into the patient's room, but he was still sleeping peacefully. In the kitchen, she found Duncan Cameron working his way through a bowl of thick porridge. Evidently he was not a morning chatterbox. He nodded in reply to her greeting and indicated a pan of porridge on the stove.

Grace's years among less austere cultures had affected her eating habits, but there was an unopened box of Cornflakes on the table and she helped herself. 'What does your nephew take for breakfast?' she asked.

He scraped the last spoonful from his bowl and swallowed it before answering. 'He likes his oatmeal with a pinch of salt. Then brown bread with marmalade or honey.'

'Tea or coffee?'

'Coffee. There's instant. Decaffeinated. White, no sugar.'

That seemed to cover the subject with the minimum of words. 'Fine,' Grace said. 'I'll give him his breakfast and his exercises and get him ready for the day. After that, I'm supposed to go and visit his doctor – Dr Sullivan, is it? And then I'll have some errands to do. Can you look after him, probably until early afternoon?'

'What day is it?' he asked suspiciously.

'Friday.'

He considered, scowling, and then prepared to launch into what was, for him, verbosity. 'I'll manage today but you'll let me away tomorrow and the next day. Caley Thistle are playing at home,' he explained. 'It looks to be a good match. And I keep the Sabbath, both services, so you'll need to pray at home.'

Grace kept her eyebrow down but it required a muscular effort. Her personal view was that somewhere behind nearly all of the world's violence lurked either religious differences or football. A world ban on professional sport and all organised religions, she felt, would go a long way towards establishing permanent world peace, but it was too early to risk souring their relationship by saying so. It would be time enough when the patient was more self-sufficient and his uncle began applying moral pressure to her to accompany him to the kirk. 'That will be all right,' she said.

They finished breakfast in silence and he began to wash the dishes. She looked in on the patient again and found him awake and with the radio playing. 'You seemed to sleep well,' she said.

She had left him in a buoyant frame of mind the previous evening but his mood seemed to have slumped again. 'It's all this damned medication.'

'I expect so. How do you feel?'

'A wee bit stiff and sore. Rougher than I did yesterday.'

'Did you go on exercising after I left you last night?'

'For a while.'

'You'll have to make progress slowly. The objective is to work each joint without putting a load on it. I'll see what I can do to loosen you up again. Are you hungry?'

34

'A bit. First I want the bedpan. I can just manage for myself it you pass me the pan.'

She gave him the bedpan and then left him in privacy while she prepared his tray. To encourage his manual dexterity she let him feed himself while she stood by to help if required. As he finished eating there came a break in the music.

'All together now,' she said.

He choked with laughter and snorted a bread-crumb down his nose. When she had cleaned him up, they hummed along with Beethoven for lack of any words.

An hour and a half later, he was fed and bathed and gently exercised. He had tried to shave himself but at such risk of slicing his face open that she had soon taken over for him. Before she left him, she said, 'Your uncle will be in charge for a few hours. I have some errands.'

He looked cautiously towards the door. 'Would you do an errand for me?'

'Yes, of course.'

'There's money in the top drawer of the dressing table. Would you get me two six-packs of lager? And if it's not too much trouble, keep them in the boot of your car. Uncle Dunc thinks that beer is a passport to hell. It's not that I'm afraid of him,' he added quickly, 'it's just that he refuses to do it.'

'I can manage that.'

'And...' He lowered his voice further and looked shame-faced. 'How about a twenty of Benson and Hedges?'

Despite her professional disapproval, she found the signs of human frailty in a depute headmaster mildly endearing. 'I'll think about it. But you're not ready to go outside yet. I assume that your uncle doesn't approve of tobacco either? What would you do if he smelled the smoke?'

He produced a full-bodied smile. 'I was going to blame you.'

She laughed with him. 'You've got a nerve, but go right ahead. I'm not afraid of your uncle. You're a bit of a lad, aren't you? Who chose the erotic wallpaper in my room?'

He actually blushed. 'I did. I never saw what it portrayed until after it was up and I never changed it. One of my aunts stayed in the room for three weeks and never noticed it. I'd forgotten it was there. Do you mind?'

She laughed again. 'Lord, no! It's a pretty paper and I've no objection to a little glamour about the place. You can put back your Pirelli calendar, if you like. I'll even hang it up for you, that's how broad-minded I am.'

'I do not have such a thing,' His smile came back. 'But you can buy one for me while you're out.'

A thin veil of cloud made driving more comfortable but it was warm enough to drive with the window down. She passed a filling station and noted that the displayed prices of fuel were not as excessive as they might well have been in such a remote area. The sights, sounds and smells kept bringing childhood memories back to her.

Twenty minutes brought her to the surgery, a new building set back from an old village street. According to Duncan Cameron, Dr Sullivan was on the verge of retiring – and had been talking about it for years. His younger partners were carrying most of the workload but Dr Sullivan had attended at Stuart Campbell's accident – probably he had been the doctor on call that day – and the case remained his.

Grace took a seat in a bright, half-filled waiting room. She kept her eyes away from the decorative National Health posters. She had no wish to be reminded of her own mortality. After a few minutes, a fat lady emerged from Dr Sullivan's consulting room grasping a prescription form and the doctor escorted Grace inside and showed her gallantly to a chair.

The doctor was a small man but tubby. His hair was silver but at least he had kept much of it. He still had a twinkle in his eye and Grace, who had few notions about the impassivity of doctors, decided that if she ever required an intimate examination she would approach one of his partners. She judged that he had passed the normal retiring age some years earlier, but his manner was still brisk and he took her through the casenotes with only occasional reference to the file.

When they had dealt with such matters as treatment, medication and the system for renewing prescriptions, and the doctor had promised to arrange for the loan and delivery of a folding wheelchair and a zimmer frame, she said, 'Doctor, did Mr Campbell give you any explanation for his accident?'

The doctor leaned back in his swivel chair and looked at her over his gold-framed glasses. Some of his brisk and cheerful manner evaporated. 'He fell off a roof,' he said. 'He does not remember how.'

She nearly abandoned the subject but some reserve in his manner decided her to pursue it a little further. 'I know that it's only marginally my business,' she explained carefully, 'but I prefer to have the fullest possible details of a patient's mishap. It helps me to picture what's happening inside the joints and muscles. Then I can adjust the physiotherapy to suit. In this case, I have difficulty envisaging the accident. I spent several years in the A and E department of a large hospital and I must have seen a dozen builders who had taken a fall off the scaffolding, but the pattern of injuries never matched these.'

The doctor had begun nodding like an elderly automaton. 'I know what you mean,' he said. 'I must admit that I was surprised that any enquiries were left to the local bobby. On the other hand, there were no suspicious circumstances. As I told Andy Wallace – Constable Wallace, I should say – the young man was very much looking forward to a holiday in Thailand. I had given him his booster shots only a few days earlier and he was in a very cheerful mood. And even if there had been any question of suicide, he would not have found it necessary to jump where there was another roof only twenty feet below. A few paces to one side and he would have had a further four storeys to fall. Also, he was perfectly sober.'

'His blood was tested?'

'Not that I know of. Perhaps I should explain,' the doctor said, looking at her this time through his glasses, 'that I was present, as one of the school governors, although I did not see the occurrence itself. I noticed that Mr Campbell took only one small glass of *usquebae*, which is neither here nor there,' said the doctor with the true Highlander's acceptance of whisky as a necessary fact of life. 'I would happily have certified that he was safe to drive a car.'

'And nobody saw him fall?'

'Not so far as I am aware.' The doctor's professional reticence had fallen away and the born gossip had emerged. 'The company was gathered where the refreshments were. The stairhead and the toilets were out of view. The first that I knew of any such incident was when somebody – a woman's voice – cried that a man had fallen. We all hurried over and looked down. There was quite a crush and some danger of another faller being pushed over the brink.'

'No handrail?'

'Not as such. The scaffolding was still around most of the building with a platform at roof level, so I suppose a taut rope between posts was considered sufficient. But at that end of the building there was a solid wall below – to stiffen the structure, I believe – and the scaffolding was no longer required.'

'So, if he had decided to jump, it would have been easiest there?'

'Well yes, I suppose so. As the only doctor present, I went down and clambered with some difficulty onto the lower flat roof. By then Mr Campbell was on his back, but that means very little. A person will often bounce or roll over, or make a desperate effort to turn over onto the less painful side. His injuries were just as we've discussed. There was little I could do except to straighten his limbs very gently and make him as comfortable as I could while we waited for the ambulance to arrive. Getting him down was the devil of a job, I recall, and the contractor had to use a... a hoist, I think it's called, to bring the stretcher down to ground level. I'm afraid that that's all I can tell you.'

'It sounds as if it was a simple accident,' Grace said thoughtfully. 'If he'd jumped, it could be relevant. I don't suppose anybody had any reason to give him a push?'

'He seems well liked,' the doctor said. 'But schoolmasters can make enemies. It seems to me... But I mustn't talk scandal, in my position.'

'Of course not.' She tried to inject a little doubt into the words.

He refused the bait. 'If you want to get a clearer picture, the local paper had a photographer there who was also taking publicity photographs for the contractor.'

'Did he take photographs of how Mr Campbell was lying?'

The doctor scratched his chin, apparently as an aid to memory. 'It was a she,' he said. 'And I would expect her to. In fact, yes, I'm sure I remember looking up and seeing her camera looking down at me. You could contact her through the paper, or through the builder. Firth Building Contractors.'

Grace smiled. 'I don't suppose it's important,' she said. She thanked the doctor for his help, shook his hand, extracted her own from his over-friendly grip and escaped back to her car.

4

Rather than retrace her route, Grace continued her circuit around the Firth, renewing her acquaintance in passing with many of the scenes from her youth. She had walked and cycled the area and, later, had threaded it in the sports cars of successive boyfriends. She forced herself to concentrate on her driving, resisting the temptation to drink in the once familiar scenes now granted renewed freshness by her long absences. The countryside was looking its summertime best, giving no hint of the severity of winter so far north.

She rejoined the main road northward only to leave it again for the few miles to Dornoch. The doctor had given her several prescriptions which she left for filling before making Stuart Campbell's purchases (other than the Pirelli calendar) plus one or two on her own account.

The pharmacist had been out of the chemist's shop for 'a minute or two', which Grace knew could, in the unhurried manner of the Highlands, stretch to an hour or more. In his absence, other members of staff were not permitted to hand out prescription drugs. It made a perfect excuse for a visit to her parents. She drove a mile to the very fringe of the ancient town to where her parents had moved when she was beginning school. It was a house of moderate size but sturdy construction standing in a spreading garden, foursquare to the onshore gales but with a view over the golf course to the sea.

Mrs Gillespie answered the door in a dress that Grace recognised as a favourite of her mother's, dating back some years but an expensive purchase treasured for special visitors. This, Grace knew, could not be for her benefit because she had given no warning of her visit other than a tentative arrangement over the phone to pay a call whenever she could escape her responsibilities. During her long absences, she had kept in touch by a series of phone calls and had received in turn frequent letters verbose with news of local doings and people, many of whom were newcomers quite unknown to her. But it had been several years since she had seen her mother and, as usual, there was a slight shock as she saw how the years had taken their toll. Mrs Gillespie had lost the slight plumpness of her middle years and was taking on a birdlike look, heading for a skinny old age – which Grace had observed often went with longevity.

Mrs Gillespie welcomed her daughter with open arms, left her standing in the hall for a moment while she dived into the kitchen for a cup and saucer from the very best tea-set and then led her into the sitting room. This overlooked the garden and Grace felt a momentary sense of change, as if an old friend had visited a top hair stylist or had a nose job. The garden had never looked so perfect and yet so natural during her years at home. The sitting room was bright with the morning sun. The pastel paper was fresh but at least the pre-war furniture was comfortably familiar.

'You remember May Largs,' Mrs Gillespie said. 'May Forsyth, she was.'

The only other occupant of the room was a woman of about Grace's age, who hesitated before jumping to her feet. 'Of course I do,' Grace said. 'We were at the Academy together. But you were a year or two ahead of me.'

The two touched cheeks and kissed air before settling together on the deep settee. Mrs Gillespie poured tea and passed biscuits. 'May's here about the garden,' she said.

'You were always besotted on plants, I remember,' said Grace. 'You made them a career?'

May Largs smiled shyly. 'I graduated in horticulture and landscape architecture,' she said. 'But what I like most of all is garden design. I don't get my hands dirty as often as I did, which I do miss rather. I've come to an arrangement with a local landscaping firm. I design and supervise their operations, including the day-to-day maintenance.'

'And very good she is,' Mrs Gillespie said stoutly. 'Your father grudged the extra expense at first, but I pointed out that May goes in for labour-saving designs. It would only be once in a blue moon for a makeover and then he could do the weeding and pruning himself between times. When he saw how much better other people's gardens looked he soon came around. You can usually tell the gardens that May's had to do with, because the colours look balanced all the year round and yet it all looks natural, as if it just happened of its own accord. I don't know how she does it.'

'You're not supposed to know,' May said. 'I have to have my little secrets or where would I be? Grace, you' re private nursing, I believe.'

'And physiotherapy,' Mrs Gillespie put in. 'What case do we have to thank for bringing you back, Grace?'

'I may be here for some time. I'm looking after a man who fell off a roof.'

'That would be Stuart Campbell,' said Mrs Gillespie.

'Now, how would you come to remember a thing like that? I thought that men were always falling off roofs, but perhaps that's only because my experience tends to focus on them.'

'There had been some gossip, so I noticed the name when the accident was reported.'

Grace's interest was caught immediately. 'What gossip?' she asked.

'Och, just tittle-tattle.'

Grace held onto her patience. Her mother was usually a ready gossip. 'But what tittle-tattle? I like to know all I can about my patients.'

'There was nothing in it and I thought it was best forgotten. Poor man.' But Mrs Gillespie's sympathy did not restrain her from repeating the story. 'It was about a year ago. One of the young girls, Mairi McPhaill, became pregnant. Her parents were from the islands. She was a bright girl, it was said, and Mr Campbell had been coaching her for a scholarship. It was put to her that he was the father and she agreed. He was suspended. Then it all blew over, I don't know why. May might be able to say – her husband's the Detective Superintendent in Inverness.'

'I do know,' May said, 'but that's not how I know. Will hardly ever discusses his cases and never talks scandal. But I was doing the garden at Canmore House Hotel and the staff were talking about it. Mr Campbell insisted that there had never been anything between them and he demanded a DNA test. The girl changed her story immediately. It turned out that the real father was one of her fellow pupils, but there's never been a wedding and the girl was sent away to an aunt in Harris.' She looked curiously at Grace. 'Why are you interested?'

'I told you. I like to know about my patients.'

May shook her head. 'No, it's not that. Not *just* that. Will always notices if somebody's being evasive and I must have caught it off him. You think there's something odd about his accident, don't you?'

Grace thought quickly and decided that she had no reason not to voice her thoughts. Medical confidentiality hardly applied when the patient's injuries had been witnessed by a crowd and recorded in the press. 'Yes, I do,' she said, 'to the extent that his injuries don't really match up to the story of his accident. I wondered what had really happened to him, because that can affect his treatment. His knees and elbows were badly broken. He says that he can't remember the fall and it seems to have been assumed that he landed on his elbows and knees. Well, maybe he did, although I've nursed builders who fell off scaffolding and the only one who landed that way developed severe arthritis in his hips and shoulders from the jolt that ran back up his arms and thighs. But there was also severe bruising to Mr Campbell's back, inflammation in his spinal cord and a bruise on the back of his head. I don't see how all that could have happened from a simple facedown fall. It's a matter for a specialist in forensic medicine, but it seemed to me more as if somebody had come up behind him and hit him on the back of the head and then, when he didn't go down or perhaps just fell to his knees, used their fists and knees to knock him over the edge.'

Her listeners did not seem to be shocked by this; indeed, they had been nodding as she made each point. 'That's really what worries you, isn't it?' her mother said. 'The idea that somebody might have tried to kill him and might still be carrying a grudge.'

'It crossed my mind,' Grace admitted. 'But if somebody pushed him over the edge they could just as easily have finished him off then and there. If they were paying off a score, it's over and done with, so I'm telling myself not to worry about it except so far as it affects his treatment. He's sorry for himself, naturally. I'm trying to make up my mind whether he also seems apprehensive.' She paused and looked from one to the other. 'You don't seem surprised or disbelieving at the idea.'

'I don't think that we are,' her mother said. 'That girl, Mairi McPhaill, has a brother who, I'm told, is still convinced that Mr Campbell was responsible for his sister's downfall and breathes fire and slaughter. And, of course, a depute principal can make a lot of enemies. Pupils that he's suspended for bad behaviour and their parents and so on.'

'That's a thought,' Grace said. 'I'm told that there were pupils up on the roof, going round with the drinks and nibbles.'

'I wouldn't have thought that they would be likely to give their depute head teacher a push,' May said. Grace was startled. It came back to her that May had always been shy and rather quiet until she opened up. She had been sitting so still that it had taken Grace only a few seconds to forget her presence. 'But there are one or two others who might have done it,' May said reflectively. 'There was a case a year ago. You may not have heard about it – it was reported in the Highland edition of the *Press and Journal* but I don't think that it was mentioned anywhere else. Two brothers, the Morrisons, had drink taken. They attacked a man in an Inverness street and made off with his wallet and his watch. Your Mr Campbell witnessed the assault. The men had been pupils of his when he was teaching in Nairn. He gave the police their names. He gave evidence at the trial and they were sent to prison. It was a bad assault so the sentences were stiff, and they were increased because the men made threats against Mr Campbell from the dock.'

Grace sat in silence for a while, glancing unseeing around the room and the once familiar watercolours on the walls. Her half-formed thoughts were taking on positive shape. 'Are they still... inside?' she asked at last.

'I'll ask Will and let you know,' May said. 'If you're interested, there were a lot of photographs taken. They might be helpful.'

'I'm not trying to investigate a crime – that's your husband's job. But yes, I would like to see them – they might give me a clue as to how he fell. I was going to try to get them through the office of the local paper.'

'Don't bother. The photographer is a friend and her husband works with mine. She'll have the prints that she made so that the clients could choose. I'll get them to you. And now, I must fly. Thank you for the tea.'

They said their farewells and Mrs Gillespie saw May out. When she returned, Grace said, 'I'll have to be running along in a minute too.'

Her mother's face fell. 'You can't stay to lunch?'

Grace knew that her mother's idea of lunch for either of her offspring would be a huge plate of mince or stovies. 'Better not,' she said. 'My patient will need me. Bring me up to date with the local news and then I shall have to run.'

'Not much ever changes around here. There's talk of a big recreation centre at the mouth of the Firth – a five-star hotel with a marina, a swimming pool, an airstrip, riding, clay pigeon shooting and I don't know what-all – but I don't expect anything will come of it. And there was a fight in one of the hotels last Saturday night. Apart from that, the only news has been births, marriages and deaths of people you probably never knew. You'll catch up soon enough.' She looked round at the clock on the mantelpiece, a family treasure that had featured large in Grace's childhood. 'I hoped your father would be here. But while you're nursing just a few miles away we'll be seeing you sometimes.'

'No doubt of it,' Grace said. 'Where is Dad? Golfing?'

'He went to make his peace with your brother.'

'Oh dear!' Grace's brother Simon had a fractious relationship with their father. Occasionally they were good companions but more often they were barely on speaking terms. 'What is it this time? One of Dad's jokes?' Their father was given to outbreaks of sometimes ill-considered humour to which his son often took exception.

Her mother looked guilty. 'I wasn't going to tell you this, but I'm afraid so. It was on the last day of the shooting season, the first of February. Your father was trying to make friends, so he offered to take Simon for a day's driven pheasants near Ardgay. At great expense, I might add. Simon hadn't had his gun out for months and he was shooting badly, so his temper wasn't quite what it might have been. It had been wet for weeks – you remember how it rained – and the cattle had turned the ground into a mass of hoofprints, all full of water over mud, your father said. On the last drive, Simon put his foot into a deep mud-hole and got stuck and with his gun in one hand there wasn't much he could do about it. He fell down on his hands and knees and got soaked and plastered with mud and the others were laughing.

'Then your father put the lid on it. You're probably too young to remember the old travelogues they used to put on in the cinema. Full of clichés ... "And as the sun sinks slowly in the west we say goodbye to beautiful Tahiti." That sort of thing. Well, your father put on the sort of nasal voice they used to use. He said, "And as my son sinks slowly in the wet he says goodbye to beautiful Ardgay." The other men fell about laughing but Simon took it rather badly and he let it show. Then he was angry with himself and he hasn't forgiven your father.'

'He may have by now,' Grace said. 'They're probably boozing together in the golf club.'

'And then your father will come home all sweetness and light and sloppy and he'll be like a bear with a sore head tomorrow. Sometimes,' Mrs Gillespie said, casting up her eyes, 'I think I like it better when they're not talking to each other.'

5

In the familiar atmosphere of a home and a sickroom, it was difficult to believe in any other explanation than a simple accident. The uncle's tainted attitude to life must have given rise to the doubts, which had transferred to her. Grace avoided the subject at the breakfast table the following morning. Duncan Cameron was uncharacteristically cheerful at the prospect of his football match and set off for Inverness in a rusting Polo while she was helping his nephew to eat breakfast.

Stuart was not cut off from the world. The only telephone in the house had been transferred to his bedside cabinet and, with surprising thoughtfulness, his uncle had purchased a telephone amplifier. This meant that, although it still pained him to bring either hand close to his ear, Stuart could make and receive calls unaided. When she had given him his morning wash and shave, she left him alone, at his request, to phone his girlfriend.

When she returned, he was in a cheerful mood. 'Elaine will be coming to visit me a little later,' he said. 'Do you think we could find some lunch for her?'

'I'm sure we could,' Grace said. The uncle had not mentioned a girlfriend. Grace decided to test a suspicion. 'Will this be her first visit here?'

Stuart's face clouded. 'Yes. My uncle doesn't approve. He thinks that the sexes should live on separate islands. And if that led to the extinction of the human race, it might not bother him unduly. It would be best not to mention her to him.'

'I won't volunteer the information. If I'm asked a direct question, I won't lie.'

'How very ethical! I wouldn't ask you to lie for me.' He paused and regarded her quizzically. 'But you could be just a little bit evasive.'

Grace pretended to be shocked. 'I'm surprised that you, a depute head teacher, should ask such a thing. What would you say if you found out that one of your pupils was being just a little bit evasive?'

He looked at her again and decided that she was joking. 'It happens all the time,' he said.

Deciding not to make any rash promises, Grace began his treatment. Mobility was improving in his major joints and, under the influence of heat, passive manipulation and such exercise as he could manage for himself, his right elbow and knee were flexing more. His muscles had lost their bulk during their idleness and she worked hard, and made him work gently, on the long muscles to build the bulk up again.

She finished the treatment for the moment, made him comfortable and was tidying the arrangement of her materials (which were beginning to take up more than their fair share of the flat surfaces in the room) when she heard a car door and then a footstep outside. Stuart seemed to prick up his ears and recognise the sound. 'Here she comes,' he said. 'Will you let her in, please?'

'Of course. Then I think I may go for a walk.' She had had some experience of nursing injured athletes who were in receipt of conjugal visits.

'Thank you.' She was left in some doubt as to which of her statements had earned his gratitude.

A neat little soft-top BMW was backed round beside Grace's car and almost out of sight of the road. Despite the continuing fine weather, the top was up. Grace had half expected the visitor to be known to her. There had been more than one Elaine among her schoolfellows and acquaintances, but the newcomer was a stranger. She was rounded without being fat; and blonde and busty in ways which, Grace was fairly sure, were both as nearly genuine as made no difference. Grace had seen the cast of features before on many girls. The full lips and large, heavily lidded eyes were unmistakable. Makeup had been carefully but discreetly applied. Despite noting a dress more suitable for a country ramble than for visiting a lover, this, she told herself, was a sexpot. Well, even a depute domini needed some recreation. Grace had seen enough of life to accept sex as a necessary and even an amusing part of it. Stuart was certainly in no condition for sexual gymnastics but, in Grace's experience, that would not prevent a determined couple achieving relief.

Her intention to go for a walk was genuine. She felt that she had been confined in Edinburgh and then indoors for far too long and the need to stretch her legs in fresh, country air was becoming paramount. She would have preferred to run rather than walk, but not if another woman was going to see her dishevelled and untidy. Grace had her pride.

Her good intention was immediately frustrated. After showing the visitor into the sickroom, she borrowed a stick with a carved ivory handle from the hallstand and prepared to set off, only to be confronted by another visitor's car entering the drive. She just hoped that this was the last visitor – with three cars taking up all the available space, the driveway was beginning to resemble the corner of a municipal car park. The driver, when she emerged, was another young woman, and almost equally attractive although not in so provocative a style. Grace had the impression that this one might have a passionate nature, ruthlessly subdued.

Grace did not want her patient's recovery to be set back by an emotional upset, but she could not help feeling a frisson of anticipatory pleasure at the thought of a confrontation between two of Stuart Campbell's loves. It would be worth postponing her walk for a while just to see how a bedridden depute headmaster coped with such a challenge in etiquette, especially if interrupted in mid-dalliance.

But it seemed that she would be denied the amusement of seeing a scratching and hair-pulling match between two rivals for her patient's hand. The new visitor produced a friendly smile. 'Are you Grace Gillespie?' she asked.

Grace admitted her identity.

'I'm Jenny Welles.' Grace must have looked blank, because the newcomer continued, 'I'm the photographer. May Largs said to tell you that the Morrison brothers are still in prison and she asked me to give you these.' Her accent was good, but English rather than local. She ducked back into her car, a late model Corsa, and brought out a box that had once held photographic printing paper.

'Good Lord!' Grace exclaimed. 'That's quick.'

'I still had all the prints that I ran off for the contractor and for the local rag – did May explain? When they'd made their choices, I got the originals back and sent them the digital images of the shots they wanted by email. And I was coming through this way to photograph the garden at Cannaluke Lodge, so I thought that I might just as well drop them in on the way by.'

Grace could almost see Cannaluke Lodge across the Firth from her bedroom window, but she guessed that Jenny had added at least ten miles to her shortest route. If Jenny Welles was motivated by curiosity, Grace's own interest was rekindled. She would have taken the visitor into the sitting room, but she was not sure how good the sound insulation between there and Stuart's room might be. Similarly, she preferred not to take Jenny round the house to the garden proper for fear of being heard from Stuart's room, which faced in that direction, or – Heaven forfend! – being suspected of spying on him and his girl-friend. However, at the western gable of the house, beyond the garage, there was a square of grass where she had noticed a table and a suspended seat for two under a small canvas awning. She led the way. The cushions looked reasonably clean and they felt dry. The sun had been on that corner for more than an hour but there would soon be shade from a tall rowan tree.

When they had settled themselves on the seat and adopted a gentle swinging motion, Jenny said, 'May told me why you have doubts about the accident and why you want to know for sure.'

'You're the first person I've met, other than the doctor, who was actually there,' Grace said. 'Except Stuart Campbell himself, of course, and he's still pleading loss of memory. Perhaps you can help me to fill out my mental picture.'

Jenny looked'up at the hills and then brought her eyes back to Grace's. 'I don't know that I can be much use to you. I wasn't looking much at what was going on, I was concentrating on taking the kind of photographs the paper and the contractor wanted for their quite different purposes and keeping half an eye open for opportunities to make a little cash on the side. But you may get more help from the photos, because the camera sees everything that's in the frame, not just what it expects to see, and I took a lot of shots. They don't cost much in digital.'

'Did you get any shots of Stuart after he fell?' Grace asked.

'Well yes, because of course that would be *news*. In fact,' Jenny said with satisfaction while opening her box and sifting through a fat batch of glossy prints, 'my agent did manage to sell this shot to several papers. And to a TV news channel although they never used it. They paid for it all the same.' She passed Grace the photograph. The camera was looking down on a flat surface, apparently a flat roof covered with some sort of tiles. A figure, recognisably Stuart Campbell, lay on its back near the edge of the roof and almost under the camera. Its arms and legs were twisted into unnatural positions. Stuart seemed to be conscious. His eyes were open and the expression on his face was one that Grace could not identify for certain. To such a scale, she thought, the differences between pain, surprise and fear were less than hair's-breadth, too minute to register. Or perhaps all were present.

'Did you hear him shout as he fell?' Grace asked.

Jenny considered carefully. The silence was taken over by the hum of insects from the flowers. 'I heard a shout,' she said at last. 'But it may have been the person who saw him fall or spotted him lying there. I wouldn't be sure, but I think that it was a woman's voice. The shout was the first thing to draw my attention but I wasn't thinking about it.'

'And you don't know who that first person was?'

'I haven't the faintest. The first I was aware of any incident was when people began a movement towards the edge and I followed them, because it becomes instinctive to see what's attracting interest. If a local crowd wants to see it, then so may a million more. And that means money in the bank to a freelance photographer.

Not that we're exactly broke,' she added cheerfully. 'I don't depend on what I can earn for my living, but I'm always in the market for better and higher-tech equipment and I don't like to ask Bob to subsidise me. My photographs may be more informative than I am. Like I said, the camera records what's there, not just what it notices.'

Grace looked at the thick stack of prints. The top two showed a throng of people in apparently aimless wandering. 'The mind boggles,' she said.

Jenny laughed. 'It isn't as bad as that. I've sorted them into chronological order. You'll see that the date and time are printed across the bottom of each. I always leave that function switched on and allow a small extra margin at the bottom so that it can be trimmed without losing any picture.' She gathered her photographs into small batches and set them out on the table. 'The first one or two – these – are wide-angle shots showing people arriving and chatting. I'd found myself a good little raised platform on a neat pile of bricks in a corner of the roof and I had a camera with a good zoom lens, so I never moved around until the accident. Then we have the contractors' chairman saying a few words. A few thousand words, to be more precise, because he was making a sales pitch. The next four shots show the chairman of the Education Committee, helped by the general manager of the contractors, filling the last hole in the roof with concrete and smoothing it down. In the next three or four, it's his turn to spout – you can see somebody yawning and several guests beginning to creep sideways towards the refreshments.

'Most of the rest are wide-angle shots of people milling around, having a drink and a nibble and telling each other what they'd have said if they'd been making the speeches and how much wittier they could have been.' Jenny had a mischievous grin. She found a place and opened a group of prints. 'This shot here shows people becoming aware of something happening. Then that shot of Mr Campbell on the roof goes in here. Finally, we have a few shots of the doctor attending to him, the ambulance arriving and the stretcher being taken down on the builder's hoist, plus a few shots of the crush, recording faces and reactions. The festivities broke up after that.'

Flipping quickly through the photographs, Grace was daunted to see what appeared to be five thousand people, though she told herself firmly that these were the same people repeated fifty times. 'You've pointed out the principal players,' she said. 'Can you put names to any of the others?'

'Heavens no! I'm not a local yet. Perhaps I never will be. I could only identify what you call the "principal players" because nobody can make a speech without telling you who he is and all about himself.'

That was true, Grace thought. She thought of another question. 'As people moved to look down, what were they saying?'

Jenny pursed her lips. 'What do you mean?'

'What was the trend? Were they saying, "How did he get down there?" Or, "He must have tripped?" Or, "Did he jump?" Or "Who pushed him?" Or what?'

'Ah! I think the trend was that he must have fallen over the rope. Which, if you want my opinion, is quite possible. When I first arrived I tested the rope, because I'm nervous about heights. It was bar-taut at that time. But there had been a light shower just before we arrived and the rope was natural fibre – hemp or sisal or something – and it must have been damp when I tested it but stretched a little as it dried, the way they do. When I leaned against it to look down and take my photographs, it was slightly slack. I had an immediate rush of vertigo and I had to get behind one of the posts to take my shots. What made it worse was that I could feel the movements of everybody else who leaned against the rope transmitted through it. I have no head for heights at all so, if my looking-down shots aren't as clear as the others, put it down to shaky hands.'

'They're very good all the same.'

Jenny paused and held Grace's eye contact. 'If you still want my honest opinion, I think you should drop it. I mentioned your interest to my husband last night. Did May tell you –?'

'That he's a detective? Yes.'

'He said that the matter had already been looked at and that you don't seem to have much ground to suggest the need for a further investigation. The Morrison brothers were turned down for probation not long ago. He also said that if you do come across any real evidence, you should let him know immediately. I'll go a little further than that. If there was something suspicious about his fall, it was probably meant to kill Mr Campbell. And he knows that, which is why he's being so uncommunicative about it. But if you go around asking penetrating questions, you could be inviting the same sort of attention.'

The suggestion made Grace stop and think but she decided that the other had been reading too many thrillers. 'I'll be careful,' she said. 'But I'll probably find – if I do find out anything – that the fall was a perfectly genuine accident and that there's an absolutely logical explanation for the pattern of Stuart's injuries. Or if it turns out that he was given a nudge, it will be an act of opportunist spite by a disgruntled husband or ex-boyfriend.'

'You may be right,' Jenny said. 'But just remember that it may not. And if there is something seriously wrong, the guilty person may know that you're heading towards what he doesn't want anybody to find out before you realise that you're on to something. If you see what I mean. That sentence came out a bit garbled.' She looked up at the sky. 'I must go. The sun will soon be just where I want it for photographing the water garden. You'll think over what I said?'

'I'll think about it,' Grace said. 'No doubt about that.'

6

The presence of all three cars in the cramped drive left no room for Jenny to turn. Grace stood in the road and guided Jenny as she reversed out into the traffic, which consisted of a young girl on a bicycle and a tractor and trailer with a load of dung. Jenny drove off with a cheerful wave.

Grace's watch told her that the morning was too far advanced to allow what she would consider to be a worthwhile walk and she was still determined not to go for a run. She returned the stick to the hallstand and retreated into the kitchen. It was the first time that she had seen that room without its usual occupant. It was as tidy and sterile as a surgery, which for a man's kitchen, in Grace's experience, made Duncan Cameron a genetic freak. He seemed an unlikely candidate but perhaps a female gene had sneaked in somewhere.

Another glance at her serviceable watch told her that it was still rather early for lunch; and the presence in the fridge of sliced ham, sliced bread and a bowl of freshly prepared salad suggested that little time would be required for its preparation. She fetched her handbag – rarely carried but a useful repository – from her room and found a fine-tipped pen which could not only write on the glossy surface of the photographs but did so with an ink that could be wiped off again with a damp finger.

She laid the photographs out in chronological order. The array almost covered the kitchen table. The day of the ceremony had been bright although she could see, from the ruffled hair and warm garments, that there had been a cool wind. The only identities that she could attach to the images were the representatives of the contractor, the chairman of the education committee, the doctor and, of course, Stuart Campbell. She printed in those identifications in small, neat lettering wherever they occurred and then scanned the other faces. It was almost a mathematical certainty that that some of them would have been known to her at some time, but she had left the area twelve years earlier and made only brief return visits since, so that faces and silhouettes would have changed and she knew that her memory had faded. Moreover, she knew well how uncertain recognition could be when the individual was taken out of context.

There was no unexpected pattern to be seen in the movements of the guests. As Jenny had said, they congregated for the "topping-out" ceremony and the speeches and then milled around, chatting, no doubt grinding axes and biting backs, while taking full advantage of the contractor's hospitality. After a suitable interval, represented by many frames, Stuart was to be seen heading around the structure intended for lift and ventilation machinery and then he disappeared. Four frames later came a shift of pattern as heads turned towards where Stuart had gone. The next frame showed a general drift in that direction. One or two figures were running.

At this point, Grace was interrupted by a knock on the door followed by the appearance of Elaine, Stuart's visitor. Her face was pink and her everted lips looked bruised. Evidently there had been some goings-on. On the whole, Grace approved. A little healthy lust might give the patient more motivation to get his limbs moving than any amount of physiotherapy.

'Are you getting hungry?' Grace asked. 'I was just about to make some lunch.'

'I can't stay for lunch, thanks. I just wanted a word.'

Elaine's voice held at least a trace of the superior tones of a woman, knowing herself to be sexually magnetic, towards another whom she considered to have been less blessed. Grace, however, realising that the other would be a heaven-sent source of information, decided not to reply in kind, for the moment at least. 'Come and sit down,' she said. She indicated a chair beside her. 'I want a word in return. I won't keep you long. But has Stuart ever told you how his accident happened?'

Elaine sat. She seemed to arrange herself carefully. 'He just said that he couldn't remember. If I asked any questions, he just shied away like I'd asked him about the state of his bowels or something. In the end, I decided there was no point me bothering. Why?'

'If I knew just what happened, I could tailor his treatment better to his injuries.'

That explanation was beginning to sound, even to Grace, a bit thin for what was becoming as much an exercise in curiosity as anything else, but Elaine nodded, looking down at the table. 'From what little he did let out, I think he accepts that he fell over the rope. Do you think somebody pushed him?'

Grace felt herself flinch. That idea was beginning to look very foolish to her. 'Lord no,' she said. 'I can't believe that anybody would want to hurt him.'

She was in for a surprise. 'I don't know about that,' Elaine said thoughtfully. 'He can be quite a disciplinarian in school, in his way. He's a pussycat, really, and he hates being forceful, so they take advantage of him and he has to come down heavily to stay in control. He got two boys suspended recently. And then there was the building contract. He used to tell me what had been going on in the project committee.'

'How exciting for you,' Grace said flatly.

Elaine made a face and then smiled, girl to girl. 'You know the way it is. You've got to pretend to be interested in what they're hooked on or they get huffy. He seems to have got right up the contractor's nose, saying the next phase of the school should be put out to tender. Some of the committee wanted to negotiate a follow-on contract based on the original rates or something like that, but Stuart had consulted a friend of his, a quantity surveyor, and he swore that the rates were already too high. Also, he kicked up hell when the architect allowed the contractor what Stuart thought was too much extra time for bad weather when we hadn't had a bad winter at all.' Elaine had already wearied of the subject. Her attention wandered to the table. 'What are the photographs?'

'These are what the photographer took that morning. They don't seem to show anything very helpful. I was just trying to put names or jobs to some of the people.'

Elaine grinned mischievously. 'So you do think that he was pushed. Let's have a look,' she said. 'I wasn't invited, but I know a lot of faces.' She scanned the early photographs. 'These four teenagers...' She quoted names.

Grace wrote in the names. 'I understand that the contractor asked for help taking round refreshments. Later on, you can see that that's what they're doing. How do you come to know them all?'

'I teach at the same place. English and Drama.' (Grace tried not to raise her expressive eyebrow. Colloquial spoken English might differ from the formal written but, even so, Elaine's grammar was not always what was to be expected of an English teacher.) 'But I haven't told you. This one –' she pointed '– Dean Murray – he was one of the two who were suspended for being a real pain. Their parents appealed and the local authority unsuspended them, or whatever you call it, but they were given dire warnings and I guess Dean's father came down hard on him. He'd been the prince of the troublemakers before, but since then he's been almost good, at least inside school. I've seen him giving Stuart some dirty looks, though.'

Dean Murray looked a typical product of a farming background – large, sturdy and cheerful with a round and smiling face. His dark hair had a central parting and was clipped short.

'Go on,' Grace said. 'You're being very helpful.'

Elaine gave a small smile of acknowledgement and returned her attention to the photographs. 'The small man with the handsome face and the posture of an ape with a slipped disc is Mr Coolie. He's the sports coach and head PE teacher. I think he was invited to the wing-ding because he's on the project committee like Stuart. The stout lady is Councillor Macavenny – she lives almost next door to my parents. The man with the pointy face like a rat and the silver Hitler moustache is Councillor Allnith. He's into everything. Oh and –' Elaine broke off suddenly.

'Go on.'

Elaine pointed to the image of a young man with bushy eyebrows and a sulky look. 'Dougie Burrard. He's a surveyor in the contractor's office.'

The lack of any obvious connection caught Grace's attention. 'How do you come to know him?' she asked.

The question seemed to catch Elaine flatfooted. She hesitated and looked away for a moment before deciding on frankness. 'No harm telling you, I suppose. Dougie and I had a thing going for nearly a year before Stuart and I got together. But Dougie had no idea how a girl likes to be treated – know what I mean? He was free enough with his money but he didn't know how to be polite or... or romantic. The end was, I lost patience and dumped him.'

There were several side issues here that Grace would have enjoyed exploring but she decided not to be diverted from her quest for knowledge. 'You dumped him in favour of Stuart?'

'There wasn't any gap, if that's what you mean. In fact, there was a bit of an overlap.' She smirked – there was no other word for it. 'Dougie wasn't any too pleased. In fact, there was a bit of a punch-up between them, but I didn't see it and it's all over now.' Elaine went back to her perusal of the photographs, leaving Grace to contemplate this addition to the growing list of people with reason to wish harm to Stuart Campbell.

'Off the top of my head,' Elaine said at last, 'I can't put any more names to people.'

'Maybe next time you come...' Grace suggested.

Elaine avoided a direct reply but Grace's words seemed to turn her thoughts in another direction. 'The reason I came in,' she said, 'was to ask you something. How much recovery is Stuart going to make?'

'Surely that's a question for his doctor?'

'No way! A doctor will only give that sort of information to a close relative. And Stuart vacillates all the time.'

Grace's eyebrow went up of its own accord. Surely what Stuart had said implied that they had not met since his accident. 'This isn't the first time you've come here, then?'

Elaine looked upward and made a face. 'It's the first

time. That uncle of his is a holy terror and he thinks I'm the original scarlet woman. I visited Stuart several times in hospital. He swung between being sure that he was going to spend the rest of his life in a wheelchair and knowing for a fact that he'd be skiing again by next winter. So do please tell me what you can.'

Faced with the polite enquiry, the pleading expression and the therapeutic value to her patient of regular visits by an obliging lover, Grace relented. 'It's going to be a long haul,' she said. 'How quickly he makes progress depends on a lot of things. Just how bad the damage is. How good are his powers of recuperation. How much he wants to recover. Whether he perseveres with his exercises, not too little and not too much, like the old advertisement used to say. And so on and so forth.'

'But at the end of the day?'

'He'll be back on his feet, I think I can promise you.'

'But how much mobility will he have? I mean, are we talking about running a marathon or hobbling about with sticks? We had a skiing holiday together in Switzerland during the Christmas break.'

Grace thought back to X-rays and the reports of orthopaedic surgeons. She conjured up the feel of his limbs as she worked them. 'This isn't for general release,' she said at last. 'Above all, it is not for the patient's ears.'

'I can promise you that.'

'I'm always ready to be surprised for good or ill, but my personal opinion is that he'll be walking quite strongly in time, though perhaps with a limp. I doubt if he'll ever run faster than a jog trot and I would suggest that skiing will definitely never be on the agenda again.'

Elaine offered no more than a nod of thanks and

made a thoughtful departure. Grace found the patient relaxed but hungry. The Vaseline and the paper handkerchiefs on the dressing table were not quite where she had left them.

7

When she crossed the hall carrying his lunch, he looked in surprise at the plate. 'We usually have junk-food at the weekend,' he said.

'Not while I'm in charge. I made sure that the larder was stocked. You need a healing diet.'

'With a heart attack to follow?'

'Your cholesterol level was checked.' Her own hunger was making itself felt and it would have taken precious time to explain that the cheese and butter were for the protein and Vitamin A content, essential to healing. His body would produce more Vitamin A from the carrots and spinach.

'My uncle's more of a mince and tatties man, cold meat only if he doesn't feel like cooking.'

Grace had learned to give way to an employer's foibles but she was not going to be dictated to about a patient's diet. 'He can eat what he likes. You eat what I give you. What did your uncle do?'

Stuart yawned hugely. 'Royal navy,' he said. 'He finished up as a CPO.'

Well, that explained the pernickety neatness and the geometrical precision in the garden. May Largs, she thought, would despise the regimentation there. The flowers probably also resented being lined up for inspection. She ate her own lunch, mostly of junk food, in the kitchen. When she had washed the plates she retired to the bathroom but decided that she was still fresh enough from her morning shower. Nothing, she had learned, distracted a patient from his recovery programme like a lack of personal freshness in the therapist;

on the other hand, the next phase of treatment would entail hard physical work and she tried to draw the line at three showers a day. Skin, she knew, was a marvellous product but surely there was a limit to how much washing it could take before it became threadbare. After all, even leather shoes could wear out.

She collected the heaviest of her cases, containing her portable electrical equipment, and hauled it through into Stuart's room. She had ultrasound equipment and an electrical stimulating machine for interferential therapy.

'I wouldn't mind one of those beers and a cigarette,' he suggested.

'I dare say you wouldn't. Do you smoke at the school?'

'Never.' He sounded shocked. 'I usually have one cigarette while I drive to the school and another in the car on the way home. Does that make me a bad person?'

She laughed. 'Only slightly bad,' she said, 'and very weak. If you're a good boy, you'll get one of each later. First, your real treatment begins. And it begins with your muscles. There would be no point getting your joints working if your muscles are too wasted to support them. We'll tune them up one at a time. First we warm a muscle area with a hot pack. Then, while the next one's warming, we loosen up the first one with ultrasound followed by an electric stimulus.'

'Electric shocks?' He sounded nervous.

'No, not electric shocks. You'll feel a prickling sensation and then a contraction of the muscle. After that we start the exercises.'

'My turn to do the work?'

'Some. But I'll be helping you. I'll tell you when to use your muscles. Mostly, I'll be flexing your joints for you, to loosen them. And a passive stretch stimulates the secretion of synovial fluid to lubricate and nourish the cartilage – I bet you didn't know that,' she added in a lighter tone. 'Passive movements will help to get your mobility back and you'll need muscle control over this new range. Later, you can exercise yourself. As your strength improves, and when the fractures are stable enough, I'll give you resistance with my hands or with weights.'

'And after today's treatment?'

'Then, if you've done exactly as you're told, you may get a treat. We can leave your bath until later.'

He smiled in amusement. She was treating him as she might a child, promising a trip to the zoo; his responses were appropriate and, in his relaxed and benevolent mood, he understood and went along with it. He was, after all, a teacher first and foremost. 'To get rid of the smell of smoke?' he asked.

'Perhaps. Or you may care to imagine that I enjoy washing your manly body. No harm in imagining.'

He grinned at her. He seemed to enjoy the mildly suggestive exchanges.

The routine went well. He was in an upbeat mood and cracked little jokes, making her laugh. When they had progressed as far as allowing him to try some exercises for himself, he was amazed by his own progress. Flexing his right elbow, he scratched his nose and said, 'That is incredible. There's nothing more maddening than an itch you can't scratch. I could never do that before. Of course, I never had such a full treatment.'

'You never had a physiotherapist all to yourself before. And you're more relaxed.' She nearly added *thanks to Elaine* but decided that any embarrassment might make him tense up again. 'Keep going but stop at the borderline where mild discomfort threatens to become pain.'

His bed was well provided with pillows. She put two of them under his knees and left him raising alternate feet off the mattress. She came back with a can of lager and a packet of cigarettes and threw the window wide open. She had learned years earlier that the morale of the patient was all-important and would outweigh the risk of damage caused by an occasional cigarette.

'That's enough exercise for the moment,' she said. 'Take your weight while I get some pillows behind you.'

When she had him comfortably raised, Stuart took a mouthful of lager and then a long pull at a cigarette lit for him by Grace. His expression was one of the purest bliss. 'Nasty, dirty, filthy habit,' he said, 'but that first one is too delicious to give up.'

Grace brought him an ashtray from the drawer that he indicated and then took a seat by the window. 'You'll have to give it up on Monday,' she said. 'Unless you're ready to defy your uncle. He'll be at home.' When Stuart looked undecided, she added, 'I'm expecting a folding wheelchair. If you've done your exercises exactly by the book, we'll see if you've made enough progress to be taken out for a little trundle.'

'Great!' He finished his beer and stubbed out his cigarette.

'Why do you let him rule you?' she asked curiously. 'Even if it's his house...'

'It's my house. But after my parents died he was *in loco parentis* to me. Then he seemed to be away for most of my teenage years when I might have got some practice at rebellion. Now I suppose the old habit lingers. Could I have another of each, please?'

While he was relaxed and cheerful might be the only time for answers. 'Maybe,' she said. 'If you'll answer one or two more questions, just as simple as the others.'

'About what?'

She decided to keep her probing gentle at first. 'Why do you rate a full-time physio all to yourself at home?'

'I hated being in hospital. Raigmore's very good, but you still feel like a commodity. I got my solicitor to raise hell. They were desperate to empty wards because of some infection, which didn't make me any more eager to hang around. The upshot was that the cost is being split several ways. BUPA and the National Health. And the contractor is chipping in. He was reluctant at first, but my solicitor mentioned the Health and Safety at Work Act and there was a sudden change of attitude.'

'I can see how there might be. Have you remembered any more about your accident?' she asked suddenly.

'No.' His mood had taken a sudden dip but he kept his tone light. 'There, I've answered two questions. Do I get what I wanted?'

'We don't all get what we want in life. You get what you need. And what you need is a bed-bath.'

'I was just going to call you a ray of sunshine,' he said, 'but now I won't.'

'That's taught me a lesson.' She laughed but his laughter in reply sounded forced.

She bathed and dried him and helped him to clean his teeth. Her watch suggested that it was still too early to begin the evening meal. 'I never managed to get my walk,' she said. 'I don't want to get your limbs working and find that mine have seized up. I think I'll jog. You'll be all right if I go out for half an hour?'

He made a visible effort not to let his perturbation show. 'Please don't,' he said. 'I... don't want to be alone.'

'You dislike solitude?'

'Hate it. And I've nothing worth reading. I asked my uncle to choose me some books from the library but he came back with rubbish. Would you visit the library for me on Monday?'

'I expect so. Wait a minute.' She went through to her own room and collected a paperback that she had just finished reading. Returning, she said, 'Have you read this?'

'Now I know that you really are a ray of sunshine,' he said with satisfaction. 'No, I haven't read it and I enjoy his books. Prop me up again, please, and then if you switch on the TV and give me the remote control, I'll be ready for when the worthwhile programmes come on.'

It was still Saturday afternoon. 'You don't share your uncle's enthusiasm for football?'

'It bores me rigid.'

Her fellow feeling for him doubled. She did as he asked and then said, 'Now may I go out and jog?'

His disquiet returned. 'Please don't,' he said again.

'You can't fall out of bed,' she said reasonably. 'You have the phone. What's going to happen to you?'

'I could have a heart attack. People do, after an accident. Stuff gets into the bloodstream and reaches the heart.'

'If that was going the happen to you, it would have happened six weeks ago.'

'If the house were to be burgled, I couldn't do a damn thing about it.'

'You have the phone.'

'Please stay within call.' He spoke firmly but there was real fear in his eyes.

She sighed. 'All right,' she said. 'Will Elaine be visiting again tomorrow?'

'I don't know,' he said.

Grace retreated to her room, changed into a leotard and began a series of her favourite Swedish exercises in front of an open window. She was worried again. Somebody had said something about Stuart being apprehensive. Had it been her mother – an ancestral voice prophesying doom? But no, the words had been her own.

She finished her exercises with unusual energy. Was this frustration, she wondered in a rare moment of introspection, or was she in a hurry to return and relieve his anxieties? But when, freshly showered and powdered, she went back to his room, she found him in a light sleep. Evidently the Elaine-induced relaxation could outweigh even his anxieties. She left him to doze while she prepared their evening meal.

Stuart's uncle had made it clear that he intended to eat out. It was late evening before he returned home. He put his car away in the garage, manoeuvring with caution, and he approached the house with careful steps, but he was perfectly in control of himself. His breath smelled of a takeaway – scampi and chips, Grace thought – and whisky. While beer was the milk of the devil, whisky, it seemed, being so much a part of Highland life, was quite permissible.

According to the radio, his team had won. His mood could be expected to be good, whereas it was anyone's guess how he would react on the Sabbath. Grace had therefore decided to tackle him on several issues which were beginning to loom in her mind. He willingly accepted a cup of tea in the kitchen. She brewed it black and sat down across the kitchen table from him.

She started with the easy one. 'I can use your washing machine?' she asked him.

'Aye.' He looked at her sternly. 'But tomorrow is the Sabbath. I do not approve of working on the Lord's Day.' His voice was hoarse as though strained by cheering on his team.

'It is the machine that will be working,' she pointed out. She tried not to sound surprised, but she had thought that by now that degree of Sabbatarianism was confined to the Western Highlands.

He seemed to accept her rather specious reasoning. 'But you'll not hang it out tomorrow. I'd not want the neighbours to be thinking that we're a household of Sabbath-breakers.'

She had heard the sound of a motorbike coming and going and once a dog had barked. She had otherwise detected no sign of neighbours but she decided to leave that argument for later. 'Your nephew needs a better diet, to help the healing process.' He looked blank. Rather than embark on a lengthy explanation about proteins, vitamins and sinovial fluid she said, 'He'll get dangerously overweight otherwise. I need to do some more shopping. Most of the shops are open on a Sunday.' When he began to draw himself up, she added, 'A nurse can't stop nursing just because it's the Lord's day. God wouldn't want it. I'll have plenty of time between morning and evening service.'

'I shall be here,' he said stiffly.

The words reminded her of another question. 'He seems very much afraid to be left alone in the house. You've found that?'

'Aye. M'hm.'

'Is he getting better or worse?'

Mr Cameron considered. 'Better,' he said at last. 'He couldn't get out of the hospital quick enough, but as soon as he was first home it began. I had an awful job with him. Terribly feared he was. I had to phone my cousin's niece in Bonar Bridge to bring me what I needed in the way of shopping. Now that there's the two of us, of course, he doesn't need to be left alone.'

8

Grace settled her patient and went straight to her own bed. When she awoke, there was no sound in the house. Evidently the two men still slept. That suited her well. She had always been a morning person, rising early and cramming as much as possible into those first few hours while her energy was still at its peak and the rest of the world left her at peace. Later in the day, her profession often entailed periods of idleness and she might read or even take a nap, but in the early morning she had both energy and control.

She put on shorts, a bra-top and trainers and left the house. Just across the road she had noticed the mouth of a small track. It led her up through a tract of mature forestry to a rough pasture where shaggy Highland cattle regarded her curiously before deciding to ignore her. Her jog became a run between well-grown conifers. She could feel her lungs enjoying the air, her muscles taking pleasure in the exercise, her joints coming free, her spirit responding to the growing sunshine as a light breeze dispelled the morning mist. When she turned, the view across the Firth was materialising from the mist and appearing in glimpses between the trees, all the more lovely for being fragmented.

In twenty minutes, she was back at the road. An elderly woman in a small but shining car took a startled look at the female figure in the immodest costume, and on the Lord's Day too, but Grace had no intention of being intimidated by local prejudices. Times had changed.

In the house, there was still no sign of movement so there was no competition for the bathroom. This was a bright and serviceable room, well equipped except for the lack of a bidet. In George Tullos's house she had found a bidet useful, not only for its intended function but also as a useful place for washing feet.

Showered and dressed and still full of energy, she put her dirty laundry into the washing machine and set the machine to work. She half expected to make some phone calls that she would prefer to make privately, so she dug her rarely used mobile phone out of her luggage and put it on to charge. Ready for the day, she headed for the kitchen. Oatmeal had been soaking overnight and she put it on to heat. She heard Stuart's bedside radio come alive. She finished her own breakfast before carrying his tray across the hallway. Stuart brightened as she entered. He was looking more cheerful than she had so far seen him. 'Look,' he said.

The movements of his arms and legs might have looked feeble to the uninformed passer-by, but Grace was pleased. 'Very good,' she said. 'But don't overdo it. I'll give you another going over while your uncle's at morning service and again in the evening.'

He could still reach his face with only one hand but he could manage to feed himself. He tucked in to his breakfast but paused to say, 'We could begin as soon as I've finished eating. Then I could have a beer and a cigarette while he's out.'

'You realise that you're showing the classic symptoms of addiction,' Grace said severely.

'Be fair. There aren't many other pleasures to look forward to while you're bed-ridden.'

Grace refrained from asking whether he didn't count the attentions of Elaine as a pleasure. 'We'll see what we can do. Then I want to get out to the shops. Who provides the household money? I want to lay in a supply of proper food for you.'

'You know where my wallet is. You may have to take my bankcard and visit a hole-in-the-wall.' He quoted the PIN.

'You're very trusting.'

'You have an honest face.'

By turning her head, Grace could see her own face in the dressing table mirror. It did not strike her as looking unusually honest. She had not seriously considered her own face in an age but suitors had, in the past, told her that it was serene, refined, even beautiful. She had taken these compliments with the proverbial pinch of salt. Now, when she looked at it beyond the mask of familiarity, it was not a bad sort of face. The features were good and added up, she thought, to an expression of cheerful goodwill under the strictly tied back dark blonde hair. Her skin was good, considering her thirtyish years, and her eyes were clear and blue. She wondered why she was suddenly seeing herself objectively after years of taking her appearance for granted.

Treatment was under way and she was working on his right knee when the phone rang. Awkwardly, because he was lying on his face, he tried and failed to reach the telephone amplifier. Grace pressed the switch for him.

'This is Ken Rosewell,' said the disembodied voice.

'Just a minute,' Stuart said. He twisted his head round to speak to Grace. 'Would you mind?' he asked.

Guessing that he was asking for privacy rather than assistance, she said, 'Of course not.' It took her a second or two to switch off her electrical instruments while Stuart dragged himself round to reach for the handset prior to switching off the amplifier. The voice spoke again. 'When are you going to get back to work for us? I know you were injured, but you can use your laptop, surely.'

Stuart reached the amplifier. Grace left the room, but as she closed the door she heard Stuart's voice begin, 'I'm not going to be –'

Not going to be what? Able? Hurried? Interested? Threatened? It was none of her business, she reproved herself.

There were sounds from Duncan Cameron's room. She ignored them and stepped outside the front door, enjoying the sunshine for a minute or two. When the distant murmur of Stuart's voice ceased she turned back. The older man was crossing the hall, dressed for church. He wished her a good morning in gloomy tones and headed for the kitchen.

The mulish expression was back. Stuart offered no explanation of the phone-call. Grace did not expect it. She said, 'I think you'll be able to manage a laptop computer before long.' He looked at her sharply. 'I wasn't listening,' she said quickly, 'but I could hardly help hearing what your caller said. Later, would you like me to bring you your laptop? The exercise might be good for your fingers.'

He shook his head. 'Don't bother.'

She resumed treatment, working mainly by touch. Closing her eyes, she was struck by how much his mobility and muscle-tone had already improved. His body felt good, even after the period of hospitalisation, well muscled and with no more than the right amount of fat. When she opened her eyes, they focused by chance on the Caller Display which was an integral feature of the amplifier. This was showing Ken Rosewell's number. Grace would never have noticed nor remembered it but for the coincidence that she had been employed for a nearly a year to rehabilitate a senior journalist's wife who been smitten by multiple sclerosis. The journalist's area code at work had been the same and Mr Rosewell's number – 3434 – was impossible to forget.

They resumed his treatment. She paid as much attention to maintaining his muscles as to working mobility into his joints. The slight wastage that had already been detectable in his muscles offended her. He had had a beautiful body, one that raised a distant response in her own, and she was determined to restore it.

Duncan Cameron drove off, in his nephew's Rover, before the treatment was quite finished. He was dressed in a stiff suit and a dark tie. Presumably his own more battered car would not do justice to the occasion or to his Sunday attire. As Grace put her equipment aside, Stuart said, 'I think I heard my uncle driving off, complete with Bible and good intentions?'

'And an odour of sanctity you could smell through a brick wall, if you don't mind my saying so.'

'Of course I don't mind. Speaking of the Bible, did you know that a whole chapter was omitted from the Book of Genesis? It only turned up recently in the Dead Sea Scrolls.'

There was a gleam of mischief in his eye but she decided to go along. 'No, I didn't know that,' she said.

'It comes very early on, when God spoke to Adam about a companion. "I shall provide you with a woman," He said, "to be a prop and a comfort to you. She will cook and clean for you, make you clothes when you get around to clothes, never grudge you a beer or a cigarette and never, ever have a headache. But –" and remember, this was a Jewish God "– but she will cost you an arm and a leg."

'"I don't think I could spare an arm and a leg," Adam said, "What could you let me have for a rib?" Now how about it?'

Grace let her laugh spill out. There was no need to ask what he meant. 'I think that you cleaned that one up a bit,' she said. She went out to her car for a can of beer and the packet of cigarettes and then hurried to hang out her now clean but damp laundry on the line. When she returned to Stuart's room, he was alternately sipping and puffing contentedly. She was tempted to ask him why he was too nervous to be left alone, but his mood was too good to spoil. Instead, she said, 'Don't spill ash on your sheets unless you're prepared for a fight with your uncle. I'm not going to wash sheets every time you want a smoke, or at all. You wouldn't need all this secrecy if you just came clean and stood up to him.'

'If you helped me into the wheelchair,' he said, 'we could go out and avoid all the fuss.'

'There's nowhere to wheel you here away from the house,' she pointed out. 'Just a narrow road and a soft verge.'

'There's a place round the corner of the house. Or you could wheel me as far as your car and drive to the hotel.'

She could have said that she was not running a taxi service. She could have said that she had never gone out socially with a male patient and had no intention of breaking the rule. Instead, she said, 'You're not ready to fold up into a car yet. I'm not having you put any loading on those joints until the healing process has gone a bit further and until I've got your muscles in a better condition to support them. Part of my job is to save you from yourself.'

'Nobody ever got thanked for that service. How long, then?'

'That depends on how good you are at doing, but not overdoing, your exercises. Not long.'

He sighed. 'You wouldn't believe how I'm looking forward to getting out and about, even if it's only to be wheeled around the garden. I haven't seen anything for months except hospital ceilings and the view from the window.'

'You have a superb view without even getting out of bed. You've got flowers and water and trees and fields and sheep and hills. Most of my patients would have given their teeth for a view like that – those who had teeth – or even for any two out of the six.'

Stuart had the grace to look ashamed. 'I know the view by heart now. I don't want to sound peevish. I know I'm lucky, if falling off a roof can be lucky, but I want variety. I *need* change.'

Grace could easily believe that. It was the only topic common to almost all her patients.

At times her job was repetitious, requiring all of her skill but little of her mind. While she performed the well-remembered motions, she had been thinking. If there was a simple explanation for how an accidental fall could result in his injuries, she could not think of it. The contradictions nagged at her and her constant pre-occupation with his physique kept them at the forefront of her mind. Her father was a respected member of the business community and knew almost everybody, but when she phoned her mother, though she received the expected invitation to lunch, it was to learn that Mr Gillespie was on a golfing trip to Gleneagles with friends and would be back late. Grace declined the lunch but promised to pay a quick visit.

There was one other promising source of local knowledge, one that needed no advance warning.

The service must be almost over. She put her mobile back on charge and hurried out to collect her still damp laundry and transfer it to the tumble drier. She got rid of the debris from Stuart's little orgy, burying it deep in the refuse sack. The smell of smoke had almost completely escaped and the wide-open window would be a give-away, so she half-closed it.

The prospect of liberation, however slight, had raised Stuart's spirits further. He made quite a production of shaving himself with only minimal assistance from Grace. He was submitting almost cheerfully to the humiliation of his bed-bath when Grace heard the sound of the returning car. Soon, Duncan Cameron looked into the room. He sniffed the air. 'That Elaine's been here,' he said.

Taken literally, the statement was true. Neither Grace nor Stuart felt obliged to mention that he was misleading himself as to when it had been true. Instead, Grace said, 'I shall be going out to lunch. I take it that you'll look after Stuart?'

'I suppose so,' the older man said. His gloom might have been put down to the aftermath of the service and a good old-fashioned sermon promising the wrath to come, but Grace suspected that, rather than cold meat straight from the fridge, he had been hoping for a cooked meal prepared by a heathen who was prepared to flout the Lord's day. 'When will you be back?'

'I'll be in good time to let you away for the evening service.'

'See that you are,' he said.

Grace stopped herself from giving a sharp answer.

She gave Stuart precise instructions as to what exercises he might or might not attempt in her absence, changed into a more suitable dress and left the house.

9

Grace extracted her car from the driveway with some difficulty. She had never been the most confident driver at reversing and her car was tucked away rather tightly in order to permit the turning of Stuart's car and that of his uncle but she made it to the road, rather breathless, without causing any damage. It occurred to her in passing that if she were going to spend many months nursing Stuart and driving a dozen miles around the Firth each time that she wanted to travel a distance which any sensible crow could cover in two, a motor-boat might be a sound investment.

Almost directly across the Firth from Strathmore, she left the road and turned down the hotel drive towards the Firth. The Canmore House Hotel had once been a substantial mansion belonging to one of the premier local families but had for some years been a very upmarket hotel. Not as upmarket as neighbouring Skibo Castle nor as expensive, but upmarket and expensive enough by local standards. The fine weather had brought out the Sunday clientele. The car parking was almost full and several family groups were sitting at tables on the broad terrace while children played on the lawns. The gardens had undergone a transformation since her last visit. She wondered why they seemed more welcoming that ever before and realised that, after her mother's words, she could detect the fine hand of May Largs in the design. Capability Brown, she thought, rather than Inigo Jones.

Inside, the bars were busy and the dining room already had customers. At the reception desk a dignified young woman with impossibly permed hair dyed an equally impossible magenta, who Grace recognised with some difficulty as having been an early teenage hoyden, seemed to be in charge. Her nametag said *Celandine* though Grace, without being quite certain, seemed to recall something more mundane. Grace asked for Derek McTaggart, the manager.

'Who shall I say is asking for him?'

'Grace Gillespie.'

There was still no flicker of recognition but the receptionist picked up an internal phone.

Derek McTaggart, when he arrived, was more forthcoming. He was a sandy-haired man of about Grace's age but already tending towards stoutness. He had the confident bearing and alert eyes of hotel managers everywhere. He bustled into the foyer, already showing the smile of the professional host. 'Grace!' he said guardedly. 'How good to see you again.'

'You too. Could we have a quiet word?'

'Of course.' Derek looked around uncertainly. The hotel was busy. He offered her a seat in a quiet corner beside the lifts. Grace remained standing. She could understand his reserve. After a protracted teenage romance they had finally introduced each other to the pleasures of physical love. The affair had been conducted in the summerhouse behind Derek's home. Despite the balmy summer air, the scent of flowers and the sound of crickets, it had been less than romantic – painful on her side, embarrassingly unsuccessful on his and reduced almost to farce by his clumsy manoeuvres with the unfamiliar prophylaxis. Their romance had faded quietly away and, with the end of their last school year, they had only glimpsed each other on rare occasions since.

'I'm not here to embarrass you,' Grace said. 'My mother wrote to me that you married Joan Buchan. She was a friend of mine and I wouldn't want to hurt her, so whatever was once between us never happened. I'm in search of local information and it struck me that a hotelier was the person most likely to have access to all the gossip.'

His face cleared. 'Of course,' he said. 'Follow me.'

He led her through the public part of the hotel to a comfortable attached cottage, which had been made out of what Grace thought had once been stables. The conversion had been carried out with good taste and common sense and any lingering odour of horses was probably in her imagination. In a small but very modern kitchen, a woman was working. Grace could hardly recognise, in the smart dress beneath a crisp apron and with hair skilfully or expensively dressed, the girl who had once been totally preoccupied with horses. That recollection, Grace thought, might be what had convinced her that she could still smell the stables.

'I've brought an old friend to see you,' Derek said. 'She's on the hunt for local scuttlebutt.'

Joan smiled warmly. If she had ever heard of her husband's earlier affair with Grace, evidently it was forgiven and forgotten. 'Can you stay for lunch?' she asked immediately. 'Usually we have hotel food, but on Sundays I like to cook Derek something that isn't on the same old menu, just to keep my hand in.'

'I wouldn't be robbing you?'

Joan laughed. 'Bless you, no. I always make too much. I was brought up on a farm – you remember? – and my mother's great fear was that one of the men might get up from the table still hungry. There's always some to spare.'

'And I know where some of it ends up,' Derek said, patting his stomach. 'The hotel business is the wrong trade for anyone with a tendency to put on weight. Do stay. And have a drink while we wait.'

'I'm driving,' Grace said, 'but I think a small shandy would be safe enough.'

'Have it at the table,' Joan suggested, 'and I'll be able to stay in touch with whatever you're talking about. Unless it's confidential?'

'Not from you,' Grace said.

There was a broad dining alcove between the kitchen and a rather folksy sitting room. This suited Grace very well. She settled into a metal framed but surprisingly comfortable dining chair. She had brought her box of photographs in with her but she laid it unopened on the table. 'I don't want word spread around,' she said. 'I hope you'll keep this confidential. I'm nursing Stuart Campbell. You know about his accident?'

'He fell off a roof,' Joan said.

'That's it in a nutshell,' said Grace. 'But his injuries don't match up with his story and he claims that he can't remember what happened. He also seems afraid to be left alone in the house.'

'You think that he was pushed?' Derek asked.

'It seems to be a possibility. He pretends that he does not want to be left alone in case he has a heart attack from a left-over blood clot, but I've told him that that's nonsense. I think somebody's put the fear of God into him and he wants witnesses around to save him from being attacked again. I could be wrong, but I don't think I am. Well, I don't want to spend weeks or months getting him back on his feet only to have him injured again. Anyway, I rather like him.'

Joan looked round the door and gave her the quizzical

look of a woman suspecting a romance. 'You do, do you?'

Grace forced a laugh. 'Yes, I do. But I've only known him for two or three days and he has a girlfriend, so you needn't start sniffing for orange-blossom or touting for the business of catering the reception. All the same, I do want to know what happened, so tell me anything you can about him.'

'I remember him when he came as a very new physics teacher,' Joan said. She gave a quick look back into the kitchen to assure herself that her pans were boiling but not boiling over. 'You'd both left by then. He was a good teacher and he could be funny with it, so he held your attention. I always had difficulty understanding anything that I can't see or feel, but he made electricity and electronics seem quite simple. I've forgotten it all since, though. What else? He was brilliant with computers. I remember once he demonstrated how you could "hack in" to other peoples' secrets, just to warn us not to use a computer with a telephone modem for anything we didn't want the world to know about. He didn't show us how to do it,' she added quickly, 'he was far too discreet for that, he just showed us that it was possible.

'He wasn't very good at discipline and his classes sometimes got out of hand, so I've sometimes wondered how he gets on as a depute head. I suppose that the extra authority makes it easier for him. I had a crush on him for a week or two until a better looking PE teacher came along. I don't remember him as the sort of person to make enemies. But wasn't there some sort of scandal later? I was abroad at the time,' she explained to Grace. 'I did a year as an exchange student of catering management in Boston.'

'That's water under the bridge by now,' Derek said.

'Mairi McPhaill got herself in the family way and at first she pointed the finger at Stuart Campbell. Rumour had it that she rather hoped that he might make an honest woman of her, because he was obviously on the way to a good career and half the girls fancied him. It turned out that a boy even younger than herself was the culprit.'

'I heard that she was sent away to an aunt in Lewis,' Joan said.

''You're away out of date,' said Derek. 'She's back and there's a wedding planned. Not to the father – Jimmy Something – but some other former sweetheart. One of many, I gather, because she was a popular girl with an affectionate nature.'

'So her brother's no longer breathing fire and slaughter?' Grace asked.

'I wouldn't know, either way,' said Derek. 'He was in the public bar the other evening, looking comparatively cheerful. He's left school now and he's working for Firth Contractors.'

The name almost passed Grace by. She was on the point of asking another question when the penny dropped. She opened her box and laid out the photographs again, still keeping them in chronological order. 'Does he appear in any of these shots?' she asked.

Derek leaned forward. 'Are these of the occasion when Stuart Campbell took his tumble? I don't think the brother – John – is anything like senior enough to be invited to that sort of a do.'

Joan came through and stooped to look over their shoulders. 'Let me see, but don't let me be longer than five minutes or the lunch will burn and the potatoes will go to mush. I don't see John McPhaill, but there are several backs of heads that could be anybody.'

'If you can recognise any of the faces,' Grace said, 'write the name over their head or across the shirt-front.'

'I know a whole lot of those people from serving in the bars,' said Joan, 'but I don't always know their names. If I scutter now, lunch will spoil. I'll have a look later.'

Derek began to scan the photographs. 'This is Councillor Allnith,' he said. 'Did you know that he's the moving spirit behind this leisure complex proposal?'

'I've already written his name in on another shot,' said Grace. 'No, I didn't know that. My mother said something about a leisure centre. Is that the same thing?'

'I think they're calling it a complex. Allnith's floating a company. He points out the nearness of the two golf courses and the airstrip and what he says is good sailing water. I'm not sure that the area could absorb many more visitors, but I suppose the leisure complex will be largely self-supporting. Have you got this chap? He's Duncan McRae. He's a civil engineering consultant or something.' Derek wrote the name across Mr McRae's white shirtfront.

'Lunch coming up in a minute,' Joan said. 'Start picking up your holiday snaps, Grace, or you'll have hot dishes on them. You can try again after lunch.'

Before she could protest, Derek shuffled the photographs into an untidy pile. She could see precious time being wasted in reading the tiny printing of times and arranging the prints into chronological order. 'If I could keep these for a day or two,' he said, 'I'm sure my bar and waiting staff could put names and a lot of biographical detail to nearly all the faces. Anybody influential enough to be invited to that sort of affair is almost bound to come or be entertained here on occasions.'

Grace felt a momentary unease but she decided that she was unlikely to get anywhere with the photographs while most of the faces were unidentified. 'All right,' she said, 'but do impress on them that this is very, very confidential.'

'Definitely,' Derek said.

'At the very least, don't tell them who wants the information or why.'

'They'll guess,' Joan said.

Privately, Grace had to agree; but in the seclusion of the comfortable cottage and the sound of children's happy voices coming from outside, she had difficulty conjuring up any sense of danger.

Back at Strathmore, she found Stuart in a cheerful mood while his uncle was still wrapped in a gloom appropriate to the Sabbath. She changed her dress and started immediately on a repeat of Stuart's treatments. She found that he was responding as well as she could possibly have hoped, his joints coming free to varying degrees and his musculature beginning to recover its tone and strength. She extended the passive exercises and set him a further small regime of gentle exercises to practice for himself.

They ate early, to allow for Duncan Cameron's attendance at evening service. When the older man was away, she allowed Stuart his treat of a beer and a cigarette and then gave him the now customary bed-bath. She noticed that he underwent the ordeal without a trace of his former embarrassment. She was quite used to her male patients responding to her touch. They were aware of her and she was aware of their awareness. Any lack of such recognition she might have considered an insult to the whole female sex, although it had never happened to date. But was there now something more personal to herself? Or was she allowing her own imagination to run away with her? Grace had never considered herself to be sentimental – indeed, she had often regretted what she believed to be her total lack of romance; but she had to admit to herself that there was something in Stuart Campbell that she found very likeable indeed.

10

Grace had never had difficulty in getting to sleep. But she was blessed – or, as she sometimes thought, cursed – with an active mind that sometimes found her wide awake and in her hyperactive morning mode before even her preferred time, morning person though she was. Her concern over Stuart's mishap offered that mind plenty of grist, with the result that she awoke when the sun was barely up and most of the world was asleep.

It was the occasion for some more exercise. She put on her shorts, slipped out of the house in silence and set off on the route of her earlier run. The weather had slipped into a typical Monday morning mode, dank with a thick mist. She extended her previous route but stayed where she could orient herself by views of the middle distance for fear of becoming lost among unfamiliar fields and strips of trees. She knew from past experience that a path memorised in one direction could look totally unfamiliar when steps are retraced.

She was on her way down, feeling pleasantly stretched, when a large, black dog appeared suddenly out of the mist and made for her.

She halted. At home and in the course of her work, Grace had encountered many dogs and had become close friends with most of them, so she had no intrinsic fear of the species. She understood animals and they took to her, often to the pique of their owners. Sometimes she thought that if she ever gave up physiotherapy she might take up a second career as an animal behaviourist. She held out her hand, palm down. Even when the dog reared up as if going for her throat, she stayed calm. The body language did not suggest an attack.

It became clear immediately that the dog did indeed mean her no harm beyond a few good licks to the face, but being jumped up against by a huge dog with muddy paws is not good for the clothes and carries risk to the elderly or frail. Grace, without pausing for thought, administered the usual correction by squeezing the dog's wrists. Years of physiotherapy had given her a vise-like grip. The dog yelped and dropped down, but to show that no offence was taken it leaned against her legs, treading heavily on her feet and panting in a friendly manner.

A shape emerged from the mist, hurrying. It sharpened into a man, small but sturdily built with a bald head and a round face in some need of a shave. His face looked well worn but the ill-assorted features added up to an expression of harmless benevolence. His clothes had seen better days or a lot of work. After a startled look at Grace's legs he raised his eyes to her face and kept them there. 'What was that about?' he asked.

'I'm sorry,' Grace said. 'Your dog jumped up on me –'

'He does that. Just squeeze his paw.'

'That's what I did and that's why he yelped. But I'd no business doing it to somebody else's dog.'

'Think nothing of it.' The man looked at her curiously. His grin, while it lasted, combined with a large and slightly reddened nose to give him the face of a clown. 'You'll be the wifie come to look after Stuart Campbell?'

'That's right.'

'I thought as much.' He took out a heavy pocket-watch and squinted at it. 'I'll need to be moving if I'm to get to my work. I'm Geordie Munro. You're Miss...?'

'Gillespie,' Grace said. 'You live near here?' They set

off walking together down the hill. The dog wandered ahead about its own business.

'Aye. I'm a neighbour of Mr Campbell's and I know him well. He got me my present work. I'm with Firth Builders. Just a general labourer, mind, but it pays better than the farms. I was minded to give him a visit.'

'I'm sure he could do with the company,' Grace said politely.

'Likely enough. But I can not abide that uncle of his. A thrawn old devil, thinks he's the king of Cromarty. If Stuart would care for a visit you could let me know some time that his uncle's away of an evening or at a weekend. He knows my number. But I'd not want to bother him, mind, if he's not feeling up to visitors.'

'I think you've missed your chance until next weekend,' Grace said. The conversation lapsed while they crossed a stile. 'Did you say that you work for Firth Building Contractors? Would that be on the school where Stuart had his fall?'

'That's it.'

'You were there that day?'

'I was there. I saw nothing, mind. There was brickies working in the bottom two floors and I was carrying away the cement bags and clearing up their mess. Mostly I was picking up after them. When a brickie's on piecework, if he lets a brick fall he leaves it lying; nobody pays him to pick it up and save it. The first I knew of it, some mannie came hurrying down the stairs and cried out would we get the hoist working, ready for the ambulance crew.'

'There was nobody working where they could see what happened?'

'Not a soul. The site agent had it all fixed so that the

high-up guests wouldn't be troubled by seeing the likes of us.'

When she got the photographs back, Grace decided, Geordie would be the man to put names to some of the contractor's staff, but there was no need to spread the word of her enquiries just yet. There was one preliminary question that should not cause a flutter in the dovecote. 'From where you were working, could you see the comings and goings?' she asked.

'Not a dashed thing. Most of the internal walls were already in at that level and the contractor had put screens in the gaps, just in case some daftie wandered off and got lost.'

Geordie, Grace thought, did not have a high opinion of the area's dignitaries. She herself had an open mind on the subject.

'Did you see Mr Burrard on the site that day?'

'Let me think now.' Geordie was silent for a dozen paces. The mist was beginning to burn off under the new sun. 'Yes, that I did. He came to check on the setting-out for the brickies. He went up to join the party just before Stuart had his fall. I mind because he handled the hoist when they brought the stretcher down.'

The dog rejoined them. It was definitely a bitch. They were coming out on the road with the three dwellings opposite. Geordie called his dog by name – Maisie – and made his farewells. He crossed the road to an older cottage, separated from Stuart's house by a bungalow that, judging by the ragged grass and lack of curtains, seemed to be empty, and ushered the dog Maisie inside. A small and far from new motorcycle waited at the gate with a heavy leather coat across the tank. Grace could not think of many parts of the country where such an open invitation to a passing thief could be offered and ignored. One minute later, she heard the motorcycle leave.

The sun managed to break through while she was giving Stuart his morning course of treatment. His left leg and elbow were still stiff and sore but in general he was making even better progress than she had dared hope. She allowed him to progress into gentler exercises under his own steam. She finished with the customary bed-bath and held a mirror for him while, for the first time, he managed to shave himself completely unaided.

'Why the pensive mood?' she asked. 'You're doing very well.'

'Well enough to deserve a treat?'

'If you're prepared to face up to your uncle.'

'I could manage the zimmer frame.'

'Not just yet,' Grace said firmly. 'In another few days, perhaps.'

'The wheelchair...'

Once again, Grace weighed up the balance between the patient's morale and any dangers entailed in letting him up too soon. With the memory of his physical improvement still in her fingertips, she arrived at a decision. She took out a pair of slacks and a light sweater along with the necessary socks and underwear and began the process of getting him dressed. She found Duncan Cameron at ease in the kitchen, immersed in a tabloid newspaper.

'Stuart would benefit from a little sunshine and a change of scene,' she told him. 'But I don't want him to take too much of his own weight on those knees yet. Would you come and help me to get him into the wheelchair?'

It took all her powers of command to restrain Stuart

from using more than a minimal amount of his own motive power, but Grace was strong and Duncan Cameron was surprisingly wiry. There was only a single, very low step at the front door and, once that was negotiated, the older man left them to it. She wheeled Stuart round to the gable of the house. The sun had just reached the swing-seat. She parked the wheelchair on the grass, beside the table.

Stuart stretched and turned up his face to the sun. 'You wouldn't believe how I've missed this,' he said. He paused. 'There's less of a view, but it's a different view. And the air's fresh. Do I get my treat now?'

'Aha!' said Grace. 'I thought that this would be the object of the exercise. Well, promise me one thing. When you've finished your cigarette, take deep breaths. Breathe all the way in and all the way out, three times. There's no point sitting with your lungs full of leftover smoke.'

'That sounds sensible. I promise.'

'You are a miserable weakling. What are you?'

He smiled intimately. 'I'm a miserable weakling. But I'll be a lot less miserable if you bring me my little luxuries.'

Grace gave him a look of mock reproof. 'I'll be a minute or two,' she said. She set off towards her car, but on the way she remembered the ashtray and turned in at the front door. She had the ashtray in her hand and was on the point of leaving when the telephone caught her eye. After a moment's thought she keyed in one-four-one and then the well remembered number of Stuart's caller. There was a very short delay and a voice came on the line.

'Daily Enquirer.' Well, she thought, that explained the mystery of why Stuart had received a business call on a Sunday.

'Ken Rosewell, please,' Grace said.

There was another brief delay. A second female voice came on the line. 'Office of the Features Editor, Gillian speaking. How can I help you?'

Grace disconnected. She went thoughtfully into her own room and put the ashtray into her seldom-used handbag. At her car, she put a can of beer and the cigarette packet into the handbag, keeping her back to the house in case Duncan Cameron was maintaining observation from the kitchen window.

When Stuart had taken a pull directly from the beer-can and was puffing his cigarette, he said, 'You never keep a man waiting for long. That makes you a pearl among women. In my experience, if you let a woman out of your sight she's gone for half an hour.'

'You've been unfortunate in your women.' The exchange reminded her of a story told her by a Rugby-player patient. 'As a schoolmaster,' she said, 'how do you feel about rude words in jokes?'

'Not very strongly,' he said, smiling. 'Words are just sounds intended to convey meanings. If people choose to be offended by any words in particular, that's their choice. I try never to offend unnecessarily, so I guard my tongue. I despise people who think that bad language is funny in itself and if I hear that sort of talk in the school I come down heavily. But if it's intrinsic to the story, that's different.'

'In that case, I won't shock you if I tell you the one about the woman waiting for a train at a main line station. Local trains were coming and going but she was too early for her Intercity. There was a machine on the platform with a sign saying, "I speak your weight and fortune," so, to pass a little time, she put a coin into it and stepped on. The machine said, "You are a hundred and ten pounds, fair haired, blue eyed and you can play the violin."

'A man was standing nearby with a violin case. "Is that true?" he asked. "Do you play?"

'"I had lessons when I was young," she said, "but I haven't played for years."

'He opened his case and took out his violin. "Let's see if you still remember," he said.

'She took the violin and started on the first few bars of a Mozart concerto and to her amazement it came out note perfect. The man congratulated her but just then his train came in and he had to go. She turned back to the machine. "This is an amazing machine," she told herself. "I wonder if it knows any more." So she put another coin into it.

"You are still a hundred and ten pounds," it said, "fair-haired and blue – eyed and you are suffering from flatulence."'

Stuart had been listening raptly, his eyes dancing. He took out another cigarette and lit it with a shaking hand. 'And was she?' he asked.

Grace found that she was enjoying herself. She fanned away a wisp of smoke that had drifted in her direction and continued. 'She found that she was experiencing a little discomfort, so she walked down to the far end of the platform. She felt better after that. "This machine is phenomenal," she told herself, so she decided to invest another coin.

'"You are still a hundred and ten pounds," said the machine, "fair-haired and blue-eyed and you are about to make love."

'"It's wrong this time," she told herself, but as she turned away she bumped into a very handsome young man. The contact started a strange rapport between them. Their eyes met, their hands touched, a current passed and, without a word being said, they withdrew into a secluded waiting room. And there they made love to end all love until he heard his train being called and he had to run.

'She made herself tidy and returned to the platform. "This machine knows everything," she told herself. "I must try it just once more."'

She broke off as Duncan Cameron appeared round the corner of the house. The older man's expression and the sound that escaped him might have been considered excessive if Billy Graham had suddenly been transported to Sodom or Gomorrah.

Stuart, caught with the can raised, took a defiant gulp. Grace picked up the cigarette from the ashtray and took a puff. It tasted like burning socks but she managed to smile.

Duncan found his voice. 'What is this?' he demanded. 'Have you both taken leave of your senses?'

Grace considered launching a counter-attack on the subject of whisky drinking but decided on a different strategy. 'Your nephew needs his strength built up. Beer provides the nourishment and also the... the bitumaceous peptides that are essential to redulate the tendulous tissues. I thought that everybody knew that.' She tapped the ash off the cigarette and took another puff. How anybody could enjoy smoking was quite beyond her.

'I'll have you know,' Duncan said in a choked voice, 'that I have the strongest objection to women smoking. And I won't have it. Not in my house.'

'I am not in the house. I never smoke indoors,' Grace said with perfect truth. 'If the owner of the house objects to my smoking in the garden I shall leave. I hope you'll be able to cope without me.'

'No, I don't object,' Stuart said.

Duncan gobbled for a few seconds while he sought a face-saving formula. 'Just see that you keep it out of doors,' he said at last. He turned and went back into the house.

Stuart's face looked unhappy. 'That was cruel,' he said. 'Did you have to slap him down quite so hard?'

Grace sighed. 'I've been in too many homes where they thought that I could be ordered around like a skivvy and I've had to learn to stand up for myself.'

'But you put me in the position of having to remind him that he's living in my house.' He was beginning to sound and even to look petulant.

'He needed reminding and I reminded him.' Grace struggled to keep her patience. 'The way I worded it, there was no need for you to say anything. Now you can go and lick his boots, or any other part of him, if you're that soft. Is this all the thanks I get for saving you from being dominated by a manipulative old man? How can a depute headmaster, presumably a headmaster in embryo, be such a wimp?'

He made a helpless little gesture and then forced a smile. 'I suppose I deserved that. No, of course that isn't all the thanks. I'm fired with admiration and deeply grateful. There's a huge difference between dealing with children who've been raised to see you as an authority figure as against standing up against somebody who had control over you for a large part of your life. What you said probably needed saying but I have an uncomfortable feeling that an era has just ended. It's been an uncomfortable era in some respects, but it was part of my childhood and I'm sorry to see it go.' He lost the pinched look and a reluctant grin took over. 'You're more of a scamp than I took you for. I was ready to grab up the cigarette and swallow it when you picked it up as if you'd been smoking all your life. You haven't, have you?'

'That was my first ever, and probably my last. Don't count on me to save your face again.'

'I won't count on it, but if the occasion ever arises again I hope you will.'

'I'll think about it. Am I forgiven?'

'By me, definitely. I can't speak for my uncle.' He reached out and put two fingers on the back of her hand. 'Let's forget it. You can't believe what a relief it is to have somebody here I can laugh with. I miss the old days, when there were always a few pals around for a drink and a joke. Half of my present colleagues are old fuddy-duddies who wouldn't see the joke anyway and the younger ones would take advantage if I let my hair down with them.' He gave her hand a pat and took his own hand away. 'How does your story end?'

'You remember it, as far as I'd got?'

'You didn't warn me that you were going to ask questions.' He smiled reminiscently. 'Station platform. Violin. Flatulence. Lovemaking.'

'So she put another coin in the machine.' Grace looked towards the house, to be sure that Duncan Cameron was not lurking within earshot. 'And the machine said. "You are fair-haired and blue-eyed. You are now down to a hundred and eight pounds. You have fiddled and farted and fucked about and now you've missed your train."'

There was a pause and then Stuart shouted with laughter. When he had his breath back, he wiped his eyes and said, 'You were right. It is intrinsic to the story. So now I know what kind of stories you can take.'

'For your future reference,' Grace said severely, 'I

109

could tell that story because I'm a woman. If *you'd* told it, you would have been referring to the male myth about women keeping men waiting around while they do nothing in particular, just to demonstrate their power. Then I'd have called you a male, chauvinist pig or something.'

'Whereas I just said that you don't keep a man waiting around. Point taken. So in return I'll tell you a perfectly clean story, told me by one of my pupils. Mahatma Gandhi, as you know, walked barefoot most of the time, which produced an impressive set of calluses on his feet. He also ate very little, which made him rather frail and with his odd diet, he suffered from bad breath. What do you think that made him?'

'Ill, I would suppose,' Grace said.

'Wrong. This made him –' Stuart paused for an effort of memory '– a super calloused, fragile mystic hexed by halitosis. And now, can we manage to get me back to bed if my uncle's in a huff and refuses to help?'

'I'm stronger than I look,' Grace told him, still laughing. 'I can manage.' She judged that his mood was good enough to withstand another inquisition. 'Have you remembered any more about your fall?' she asked.

He shook his head brusquely. She nearly abandoned the subject but decided that a light approach might still succeed. 'From what I hear, you were a pain in the neck to the contractor. I expect that one of his staff gave you a push.'

He gave a laugh that she thought fell within the definition of 'mirthless'. 'No way,' he said.

'How can you be sure?'

'I'm sure.' He thought for a moment. He put out his hand towards the cigarette packet but withdrew it again. 'It just wasn't like that,' he said. 'The contractor doesn't attend project committees. I pointed out to the architect where I thought the shortcomings were and he promised to look into each one. Usually, he said that he already had it in mind. I don't suppose Firth Contractors even knew where the comment originated.' He yawned and stretched. 'It's been a grand interlude and I've enjoyed every minute of it, but it's been tiring. I didn't think that I'd ever long for my bed again but it begins to seem attractive.

In the event, Duncan Cameron emerged from the kitchen and lent a hand, silently, glumly but effectively. To make amends, Grace took over the preparation of lunch.

11

Grace had left the number of her mobile phone with Derek McTaggart. He phoned her on the Tuesday morning to say that the employees of the hotel had filled in as many names on the photographs as they knew. He added, hesitantly, that they had been helped by some of the bar customers. Grace made an awful face at the phone but it was too late for argument. She disconnected. In the hall, she met Duncan Cameron and hastily straightened her face. It seemed that all her repeated demands for caution, secrecy, discretion, confidentiality and every other word in the thesaurus had gone in one ear and, unlike the secret itself, out the other.

Her impulse was to drive to the hotel straight away, but Duncan Cameron had suddenly decided that he had urgent business to attend to and she only had time for a quick run up the hill to stretch her legs before he left. After that, she was stuck. Stuart, however, although still refusing to be left on his own, was making excellent progress so that she managed to get him into the wheelchair without endangering his recovery. A hazy sun was spreading warmth and they spent an afternoon of mutual contentment in the garden. Grace said not a word when he smoked his third cigarette over his second can of beer. Stocks were in danger of becoming depleted but the patient was happy.

It was mid-morning on the Wednesday when, after her usual exercise run, a shower and hurrying Stuart through his toilet and an abbreviated version of his treatment, she managed to drive out. Stuart was aggrieved that he would miss his little treats for a day but she reminded him that into each life a little rain must fall. Grace's mobile phone had assured her that her parents and the McTaggarts would each welcome her to lunch, but she had a very good idea where the better meal was to be obtained. Additionally, her father would be at home and before picking his brains of his extensive local knowledge, she wanted the photographs in her hand. She set off clockwise around the Firth.

She found herself following a furniture van along the southern firthside road with no room to pass until Bonar Bridge, then along the north side it seemed to be tractors and trailers. The hotel, in comparison, was set in the weekday calm suited to an establishment that depended on passing and weekend traffic and the overflow from nearby Skibo Castle. As Derek had directed, she parked behind the hotel and knocked on the door of the attached house.

Joan admitted her. 'Derek will be busy for half an hour,' she said. 'The VAT inspectors have been here. Derek set out your snaps on the dining table.'

Grace was impressed. The photographs had been arranged in their chronological order. Almost every face was now identified and somebody had gone to the trouble of repeating the names whenever an individual reappeared. Additionally, two pages of A4 paper were covered by notes about those individuals, set down in the same neat script. 'Is this your handwriting?' she asked.

Joan had taken a seat opposite, awaiting questions or comment. She nodded. 'I got the bar staff to jot down what they knew about each person, but you couldn't have read half their writings and it needed tidying. I had a quiet hour late last night while Derek was watching some sitcom that always bores me stupid, so it filled the time for me.'

'Well, I couldn't be more grateful. But I did ask you to keep it confidential.'

Joan's face clouded. 'I told them over and over. But you know what bar staff are. Part of the job is to make the customer feel at home, so they're always in need of topics of interest. If somebody utters the right word...'

Grace felt slightly hollow but decided that she was probably worrying about nothing.

Joan was called away to some emergency among the housekeeping staff. Grace began a study of the fresh data but the pattern was one of confusion. She could see a tedious period of analysis ahead, drawing plans and listing personal contacts, with no certainty of a useful conclusion. The ideal methodology would be to create a computer program that could reproduce the pattern of human movements, but the only person she could think of who would be capable of such an exercise would be Stuart himself and she could see no chance of gaining his co-operation.

She was interrupted by the return of Joan to say that Derek would meet them in the dining room. Lunchtime trade was slack but there were several other parties in the room so that discussion of the photographs had to be limited. Grace, however, could think of very few questions to ask until she could digest the fresh information. She could only reiterate her thanks for the help and, for whatever it was worth, her plea for confidentiality. The lunch was *cordon bleu* and accompanied by a glass of white wine and an exchange of news about former schoolfellows. It was a pleasant social interlude but took her no further forward.

Back on the road and heading for Dornoch, she was pensive until, passing Skibo Castle, she realised that she had collected a tailback. She pulled into the mouth of the castle driveway until the tailback had cleared and then kept her mind on her driving until she was safely parked near Dornoch Cathedral. She did some minor shopping before driving on out to her parents' home.

Her mother made an attempt to force another lunch on her while she was still exchanging greetings with her father, but before long the latter managed to carry her off to the converted boxroom which he called his study. This was a cold and perpetually untidy space furnished largely with furniture discarded from other rooms, yet somehow presenting a cheerful and homely aspect. Any disadvantages were offset by a fine view over the golf courses. He settled in his desk chair and adopted his favourite posture with his heels up on the low window-sill and looking out towards the sea. 'You'll take a dram?' he asked, but it was barely a question.

She recognised the invitation as a signal either that she was at last recognised as an adult or that he had something serious to say. 'A very small one.'

He produced a bottle of twenty-year-old malt from a desk drawer, poured and added water from a small jug. He prepared a second glass for himself with rather more whisky and less water. 'So,' he said. 'You're looking into how your patient came to dive off the roof of his school extension.'

'Mum told you that?'

'And several other people.' He turned his head to look at her seriously. 'You need to be more careful.'

'I know,' Grace said. The same thought had been in her mind.

'Yes. You don't want to get a reputation as a trouble-maker.'

That was an aspect that had not occurred to Grace. She tucked it away in one of her mental pigeonholes for

116

later consideration. 'I'll be careful,' she said. 'But I can't just leave it. My patient can't or won't say what really happened to him. I'm sure that it's because he's been threatened. The threats must have been genuine and serious, because not only is he not helping to explain his accident but he refuses to be left alone in the house.'

Her father lowered his feet and turned to face her. 'In that case, you may be doing exactly what he wouldn't want you to do.'

It was Grace's turn to look out of the window. A man was driving off from a tee in the middle distance. He had quite the worst swing that she had ever seen. When his drive had been topped into the gorse, she said, 'I'll try not to. And I'll carry the can for it if there's any can to be carried. Sometimes what people want isn't what's best for them. I may not do anything with whatever I can find out – that's a decision I'll have to take in the light of what, if anything, it turns out to be – but I want to know, because what happened to the patient has a big effect on the treatment.'

Her father looked doubtful but he said, 'I can understand that, just.'

'Then help me if you can.' She opened her envelope and produced a selection of photographs. 'These are the shots that the photographer – May Largs's friend Jenny – took at the topping-out ceremony. It seems logical to work backwards from the point at which Stuart disappears from the picture. A shot or two later you see people moving towards where he fell and then some shots of him lying on the roof below.' She handed over one of the prints. 'This is the last but one frame that he figures in. He's shaking hands with Councillor Allnith.'

'I hope that he counted his fingers afterwards,' said her father. His face darkened. 'I wouldn't trust that man

117

as far as I can spit, and I never was a very strong spitter. Well, Allnith's due to get his fingers burnt and I think it's just going to happen. He's the moving spirit behind this damn silly Recreation Complex, or whatever they call it. He bought the land himself and now he's trying to raise capital to get started. The closing date for the share offer is only a week off but I don't think any of the locals will be interested.'

'A white elephant, you think?' Grace ventured.

'Whiter than white. So white that it will shine in the dark. Tourists come to Dornoch for the golf. They drive here or fly to Inverness and hire a car. There's no call for a marina – nearly all the yachts go through the Caledonian Canal and any that pass it by and come this far north are on long passages to Orkney and Shetland. If a yacht wants to pay a visit anywhere on this part of the coast, it can call at Brora or Helmsdale. Dornoch Firth's inaccessible to most of them above the low bridge. He's making great play with the availability of the airstrip, but I'm told that the chances of the airstrip being available for planes coming to a Recreation Complex are nil.'

'And,' said Grace, 'any golfer who drags his family to this out-of-the-way spot has to be much too selfish to pay for several days membership of an expensive leisure centre for them?'

Her father looked at her sharply. Grace was dragging up an ancient family grievance. 'I'm not sure that I care for the way you put that,' he said, 'but in principle you are probably right. General opinion, locally, is that there just won't be the market. That point was made during the public meeting that was held, but the man from the Planning Inspectorate didn't seem convinced and he said that, anyway, the financial viability didn't fall within his remit. Allnith's had brochures produced which seem to make a good case. He seems to be interesting money from down south – including some from sources which, from what I hear, are highly suspect. If the project doesn't come off, he may find himself in hot water.'

'Interesting,' Grace said. 'But I don't think it can be relevant, because in the next shot Councillor Allnith's still in the foreground, scratching his ear with one hand and his bum with the other, and Stuart is just vanishing in the direction of the stairs. The Councillor doesn't disappear until the movement of the guests suggests that Stuart had already fallen, which I suppose provides him with a good alibi.'

Mr Gillespie was leafing through the photographs. 'I see that Councillor Macavenny was there. I don't see her in those last pictures, but maybe she'd moved outside the frame.'

Grace took another look at the stout, bland figure. The name was familiar although she could not remember ever setting eyes on the lady. 'She doesn't look the type to give a schoolmaster a push off a roof.'

'None of them does,' said Mr Gillespie, 'and I don't suppose that she did. She also doesn't look as if she's still sowing wild oats, but there's no doubt in anyone's mind, not even her husband's, that her second son was fathered by a minister who came in to take the services when the Anglican vicar was carted off with appendicitis.'

'Really?' Grace was tempted to follow up the savoury scandal but she decided that she must stick to the business in hand. 'But that doesn't make much of a motive.'

'That's only one of a number of peccadilloes.' He paused and lifted the bottle. Grace shook her head. He topped up his own glass. 'The point, if there is a point, is that she is quite sure nobody suspects a thing. That creates a situation in which she might do anything to protect a secret which is already a favourite topic of talk over the teacups and around the town.'

Grace found the Councillor's name on the page of notes from the hotel, but there was no disparagement of the lady's morals, just a list of her committees and interests. 'You're not pulling my leg?'

'Certainly not,' her father said indignantly.

'Then why has nobody else mentioned all this?'

'I would suppose because there is an unspoken conspiracy, which is the same reason that she thinks her secrets are still safe. The fact is that she is a very useful and public spirited council member and had done a great deal of good. She's very popular. In fact, you could say that she was much loved.' (Grace looked at him sharply. He was hiding a smile. It was that impish sense of humour again.) 'That being so, her affairs only illuminate her with the same glow that shone on any of the great courtesans of history.'

Grace was becoming both horrified and intrigued. 'But, Dad, what do they see in her? She's stout and she's ugly.'

Mr Gillespie had picked up one of the shots that featured Councillor Macavenny laughing with a small group of men. 'I don't know,' he said. 'She's put on a bit of weight, but she's not alone in that. And a still photograph doesn't do her justice. She has an animation, a *joie de vivre*, that makes you forget that she looks like the back of a bus.'

'Dad, you haven't –?'

'No, certainly not.'

They spent most of another hour poring over the

photographs and the notes patiently prepared by Joan McTaggart. Mr Gillespie filled in some gaps in the notes and attached a name to a face previously unidentified. None of this seemed to Grace to take her any further but she was at least becoming more familiar with the few facts that were emerging.

Grace set off back to Strathmore rather later than she had intended but the road made it easy for other traffic to overtake and she refused to speed up more than slightly. Her shortest route lay over the long, low bridge on the way south to Inverness, but at the southern end of the bridge she turned off at the roundabout and followed the twisting road along the south side of the Firth. The sun had vanished behind grey cloud and there was a thin drizzle. A cold breeze was whipping up small whitecaps on the water.

She had left the traffic behind. Before her twisted the open road, rarely visible for more than a hundred yards ahead, between ranks of mature silver birches. Her mirrors only showed her a single Land Rover following uncomfortably closely behind, as if awaiting a chance to pass. After several miles, she tired of the unwanted company. She was watching for a lay-by or a broad verge where she could pull aside and invite him to overtake when the other driver suddenly pushed to get by on the approach to a right hand bend.

There was room. There was patchy visibility through the hedgerow. Grace held close to the left-hand verge and was ready to brake sharply if another vehicle should appear suddenly ahead. There was distance to spare but the other driver might panic.

The road remained clear but the other driver misjudged his distance and pulled sharply across. Grace braked hard. The road was slippery with the first wet after a period of dry. She almost made it but the rear of the Land Rover caught her front bumper and the corner of her wing. With the sound of unhappy metal came a jolt which, added to her braking, was enough to break, for one vital instant, the car's hold on the road and her grip on the wheel.

There was no time for reasoned thought, only for gut reaction. Grace found herself heading for the first of a pair of trees. The car's balance was too precarious for any attempt to wrench round more tightly. The sun had chosen that moment to find a chink in the clouds and was confusing her vision by flickering between the branches. The second tree looked the flimsier of the pair. She pressed the wheel to the right and just managed to brush past the first tree and then, as the only alternative to hitting the second square on, pulled left. A wire fence checked her speed as she scraped between the two trees. Fence posts snapped off so that she was brought to a gentler halt than might have been, but the car dropped several feet into a field before being dragged to a halt.

The jerk was enough to trigger the single airbag. Grace, much shaken, was pinned there while the airbag slowly deflated. Her heart thumped in her chest and the inside of her mouth felt like sandpaper. Her engine had stalled and she could still hear the noisy engine of the departing Land Rover.

12

The rumble of the Land Rover died away. Its driver might even have been unaware of the collision, though Grace found that hard to believe. She was left with the death rattle of her own car, the click of cooling metal, a hissing that might be steam, a dripping sound and another that might have had an electrical origin. She reached hastily past the airbag and turned off the ignition.

She could have sat there for long enough, bruised, winded, pinned by the slowly deflating airbag and disoriented by events, but for the arrival of an elderly farmer who had been walking the fields and tree strips in search of an errant cow. He had seen enough of the incident to satisfy him that Grace had been the victim of some criminally careless driving. He arrived at a slow canter, seething with indignation. He accepted her assurance that no bones were broken and dragged open her door with a long groaning sound. He helped her out onto the wet grass, which immediately soaked through her thin shoes. The sun had retreated again and the wind seemed to blow clean through her. The car, Grace's cherished friend and companion for several years, had taken the brunt of the damage. Most of the panels were scratched or badly dented and one of the front suspension units had collapsed. Grace suspected that the car might be a write-off.

She was not quite sure that she could pass the breathalyser, but it took her some minutes to assure the farmer that she did not want the police. In any event, neither of them had observed even a single digit of the Land Rover's registration. However, he did have the number of a local taxi-driver off pat, having lost his own driving license, he told her, due to a minor accident after a family wedding. Grace used her mobile phone. The taxi-driver also ran a local garage and promised to recover the car and make a report on its condition.

Grace's return to Strathmore by taxi caused little concern to Duncan Cameron. Such mishaps, he seemed to feel, were the prerogative of woman drivers. But Stuart, though he tried to hide it, was very much concerned. He asked a single question about Grace's state of damage – was she hurt? – and then began an inquisition as to whether the accident had in fact been accidental. Grace was beginning to ask herself the same question, but Stuart's recovery would not be helped if his anxieties were exacerbated. She assured him that it had seemed to be just one of those unfortunate results of an error of judgement. Why had the other driver pulled in? They were approaching a half-blind corner. Was any other traffic approaching? None, but the other driver might not have been sure of that. Had she seen the other driver? Just a glimpse of a figure in a woollen hat. Had the police been called? No, Grace understood that there was no obligation to call the police if nobody was injured.

She escaped for a while to phone her insurers. Later, when she came to give Stuart his treatment and his bath, she found that her claim to be unhurt had erred on the side of optimism. Bruises and strains which she had hardly noticed at the time and could ignore while at rest made themselves noticed as soon as she began work. She tried to hide her discomfort, but Stuart was well used to their routine by now and as sensitive to changes in the contact between them as she was. He soon detected the shifts that she made in order to spare her bruised muscles. When he challenged her, she confessed to some aches and pains but made light of them.

'I'm not sure that I believe you,' he said. 'I should have noticed earlier.' His contrite expression she suddenly found rather appealing. Then he smiled. 'You're as much in need of therapy as I am,' he said. 'Hop in beside me and we'll massage each other.'

'Don't you wish?' she said lightly, although the suggestion was not without appeal. 'Anyway, what would Elaine say?'

'She won't be around any more,' Stuart said. She sensed that his emotions were mixed. Wounded male pride and loss of sexual privileges were fighting with a realisation that Elaine might not have been the perfect companion for more than an occasional passionate encounter. 'She phoned while you were out. A Dear John phone call, if there is such a thing. She didn't much fancy being in any kind of relationship with a man who might have to hobble through the rest of his days. But she wished me a full recovery and hoped that I'd find happiness with somebody, a woman I presume, who could tolerate a cripple. She didn't put it quite like that, but that was the gist of it.'

Grace gave him a covert but keen glance. He looked as though his heart would survive the disappointment even if his pride were a little dented by the rejection. 'You're showing insultingly little faith in my professional skills, the pair of you,' she said lightly. Part of her felt guilty at having been quite so frank with Elaine while another part of her mind felt relief at having wrenched Stuart out of the clutches of one who she could only consider to be a thoroughly unsuitable woman.

Stuart matched her tone. 'You're an angel of mercy and an inspiration to us all,' he admitted. 'I never expected to make so much progress so quickly. Seriously, though. And honestly. How am I going to finish up?'

'Seriously and honestly,' Grace said, 'I expect you to be able to beat me at tennis next spring.'

If Stuart had asked the next question, she would have admitted that she had never played tennis in her life and that her hand-eye co-ordination, as tested at table tennis, was more than slightly suspect, but the question went unasked and Stuart seemed satisfied. He made no attempt to relay the doubtful implication to Elaine. Instead, he said, 'You can use my car, meantime. I suppose you'll have to wait for your insurers to confirm that yours is a write-off before you can replace it?'

'I could probably afford to go shopping now,' she said. 'I don't aspire to anything new or top-of-the-range and I've been leading a thrifty life. But there's no hurry, if I can borrow yours. I think I'll wait until you're fit to sit in the passenger's seat. You can come and help me to choose the right one and make sure that I'm not ripped off. It won't be long now.'

Stuart looked doubly gratified.

In an area where everybody knows everyone worth knowing and a taxi-driver is ahead with the news, word travels fast. Grace's mother was on the phone within two hours in need of reassurance. Grace took the call in her bedroom. She had only just managed to convince her parent that she was unhurt and adequately insured and to finish the call when her mobile sounded again.

This time the caller was Derek McTaggart. 'Are you all right?' he asked.

126

The term 'all right' was capable of elastic interpretations. 'I'm fine,' Grace said. 'How did you hear?'

'Somebody arrived by taxi. The driver told him. Listen, are you still gathering titbits about people who were up on the roof when your patient took to the air?'

'I suppose so. Yes.'

'Stories keep turning up in the bars. I think word must have got around. That boy, Dean Murray, he's been suspended from school again.'

'What did he do this time?'

'He seems to have fallen foul of the headmaster. The head – Mr Paterson – is an elderly fusspot. He comes here for a meal now and again and the staff dreads his arrival. Nothing is ever quite right for him. The story this time is that he was constantly complaining that his classroom was hot and stuffy and telling the janitor to turn up the extractor fan. The janitor kept telling him that it was as high as it could go but that didn't make any difference, the complaints continued. Paterson has a marmalade cat of which he's very fond. The boy Murray's sister had a rather similar soft toy, a marmalade cat, so young Murray took that and tacked it up, spread-eagled across the ceiling grille of the extract fan. I'm told it looked exactly as if the headmaster's cat had been sucked up by the power of the fan. When Paterson saw it he nearly choked and Dean Murray was on the way home within two minutes.'

Grace spluttered with laughter. Dean Murray could not be all bad, perhaps more of a prankster than an evil-doer. Then she thought again. The prank had no significance in itself but it did mean that Dean Murray would have been at leisure that afternoon. In the photographs he had looked quite capable of handling a vehicle. 'You wouldn't happen to know whether he has access to a

Land Rover? Or whether a Land Rover has been stolen locally?'

'I'll ask around. His father does something agricultural, so I wouldn't be at all surprised.'

'Is that the lot?' she asked.

'The word is that Councillor Allnith has money problems. They're saying that he's become very slow to settle his accounts. And your patient's lady-friend came to dinner last night with Doug Burrard, so they're back together again. But he needn't think that he's home and dry, because she's also been seen with Duncan Macrae. She seems to be quite a girl. I think that's all. I'll let you know if we hear anything else.'

'Thank you.'

She relayed the story of the marmalade cat to Stuart, who chuckled and said 'Young bastard!' in a tone combining amusement with tolerant irritation.

In her bed that night, waiting for sleep to overcome the aches, Grace mentally replayed the accident. *Had* it been an accident? It was a worry that her interest in Stuart's fall had become common knowledge. Just as sleep came over her she had a momentary thought. While Derek had been speaking to her, had she or had she not heard for a few seconds the sound of voices and laughter, as though somebody had opened a door from a bar and looked into the office. She must have been mad to think that she could keep her interest a secret. Then she remembered Councillor Macavenny and she began to wonder whether there was such a thing as a secret in the close-knit community.

For the next two days, Grace lived in a state of indecision. What resembled an attack on her had very probably been an accident. Similarly, Stuart's fall might have been accidental. In which case, she was seeing a lion in every bush, snakes in all the grass, a gentleman of colour in every woodpile, all her metaphors hopelessly garbled and her fears quite illusory.

The weather remained clouded over. Nevertheless, Stuart managed to persuade her to wheel him outside. Despite the turning of her healing talents on herself, her limbs were stiff and only the fact that he was able to support more of his own weight made the feat possible. Stuart enjoyed his beer and a cigarette. His uncle, out of tact or to avoid possible conflict, remained indoors. Grace, from her seat on the swing, could see a great swathe of hills cloaked with forestry and occasional fields. Sometimes a mental picture thrust itself forward, of a rifleman somewhere among that emptiness drawing a bead on her through a powerful telescopic sight, but then she laughed at herself for her hyperactive imagination. Any sensation of being watched was undoubtedly in her imagination.

On the Friday morning, the sun was back and the world looked different. It was not a world in which teachers got pushed off roofs or physiotherapists were shunted off roads. On the contrary, it was a smiling world in which accidents might happen but the injured would heal and exercise might safely be taken. It was a world in which romance might reasonably be expected to blossom, but, she wondered, what had put that thought into her head?

She gave Stuart his morning treatment with special care. He seemed to respond – not just in the easing of his joints and the improved muscle-tone. When she touched his skin it was as if his skin had touched her hand. There was undoubtedly building up between them a sexual tension that could almost have twanged. If this continued, professional ethics might force her to hand over the case to another practitioner. She hoped not, and yet... She was relieved when the silence between them was broken.

The radio had been relaying a discussion programme, softly. She had not known that he was listening to it, but he reached out suddenly and killed the sound. 'To think,' he said, 'that those ignorant sods are being paid to bastardise the English language. "Basically" every fifth word.'

'And "Actually".'

'Yes, that too among many. I do try to encourage our pupils to leave school without any misapprehension that the more and longer words they use the wiser they'll seem.'

'Admirable,' Grace said, 'but I think you're flogging a dead horse.'

'Perhaps. But some dead horses need flogging.' Stuart produced his sudden grin, the one that wrinkled the corners of his eyes and caused a strange flutter in Grace's insides. 'The native Americans have a saying that if you find that the horse you're riding is dead, the first thing to do is to dismount. Knowing the Education Authority, their approach would be to appoint a committee with the objective of re-classifying the horse as "living impaired".'

'In the National Health,' said Grace, 'they'd probably hire an outside contractor to ride the horse. Or provide additional funding to re-train it.'

They laughed together. 'How much better a world it would be if you and I were in charge!' Stuart said.

'True. I'm going to leave you now to exercise for yourself. Don't overdo it. I've missed out on my own exercise for too long and I want to work off the last of the stiffness from my accident. You'll get out into the garden later.'

Her shorts and her bra-top had both been washed and neither was quite dry, but she was not in a condition to be overly vigorous. She changed into a t-shirt and a lightweight skirt, slipped her mobile phone into her pocket almost as an afterthought, just in case there were others who wanted to enquire after her recovery, and left the house.

13

The morning was even sweeter than she had thought. There was still dew on the ground, releasing the scents of the wildflowers, but the sun's feeble morning warmth was becoming stronger. The view across the Firth, when she cared to turn her head, was familiar but breathtaking. Grace first walked and then, as her muscles loosened, moved into a gentle jogtrot, swinging her arms. She was stiff, but somewhere ahead, just out of reach, lay perfect fitness.

While her muscles worked, she had time to think. She thought about her car. The advice from the garage was that, if repaired, its value would be less than the cost of the repair. Economically, it was a write-off and her insurers could be counted on to see it that way. When they agreed, or sooner if she had need of a car of her own, she would have to go shopping with Stuart. Her male relatives would certainly want to force their advice on her but their taste in cars tended towards the expensive and sporty. She knew what she wanted – a vehicle with carrying capacity which also must be reliable, economic to run and above all cheap to buy and insure. It would probably eviscerate her bank account, but she was being well paid and she had no other extravagances in mind. In due course, the insurance would replace the money, possibly with a bonus on top. Until then, she could manage. Stuart was still offering her the use of his car – over the loud objections of his uncle, who looked on its occasional use as his perquisite.

The paths and tracks were becoming familiar to her. She climbed through a strip of forestry, all larch and freshly green, skirted a small field where a dozen sheep ignored her in their supercilious way and passed a newer, mixed plantation of conifers and hardwoods. She came out among mature pines and thin heather, all looking much as the original Scottish forests must have looked in pre-history. Her mood was placid and reflective, which made what followed all the more shocking.

Where the mature conifers were at their thickest, a man jumped out from behind a lone wild holly and made a grab for her. She recalled afterwards that he was stocky and he was wearing a dark ski mask.

After more than two days of wondering whether she had been the victim of an attack, Grace had an instant surge of adrenaline. Her reactions were rapid and instinctive. Faster than thought, her jog became a sprint.

If she had been heading downhill she might have had a chance, but the track had been climbing and the man had emerged from his hiding-place while she was passing by. She had already begun to tire and a few strides, flat out but uphill, were enough to remind her that a car smash is not good training for a sprint. The man caught her before she had gone ten yards and grabbed her by the arm. Her training had not equipped her to deal with an aggressor. She let him swing her round while she tried to bring up her knee to his groin, but he interposed his own knee and then, without pause and without uttering a word, he punched her hard in the stomach.

Grace had no time to tense stomach muscles that were still weakened by the punch from her airbag. She folded immediately. Her whole consciousness was focused on the need to draw breath soon, before she suffered brain damage or death. She was no more than distantly aware of being manhandled, pulled about, rolled over and dragged along the ground. Her heartbeats pounded in her ears and her eyes refused to open.

Breath began to return but was immediately muffled. One of her feet was cold. She snapped back to alertness and pain. Her wrists had been tied behind her back – with binder twine, she discovered later – so tightly that her fingers were already losing sensation. She was seated with her back to a tree and the loose ends of the twine were knotted together on the far side. One of her trainers had been removed and her sock had been pulled off and stuffed into her mouth, too tightly for her to have any chance of getting her tongue behind it. In her desperate oxygen deprivation, she wanted to draw great gulps of air through her mouth but her nose was all that she could use. She could still feel her heart pounding.

The man loomed over her, his image swimming in her watering eyes. 'A warning was not enough for you,' he said. His voice was deep with more than a trace of the Highland lilt. 'You're still poking this nose into what need not concern you.' He took hold of her nose and she began to suffocate. 'Now, if folk get hurt, it's down to you. When we've done what has got to be done, I'll be back. You'll still be here.' His voice paused. Grace managed to blink the tears from her eyes. From his voice and what little she could see of his face, she thought that he was grinning. 'I'll enjoy it but you will not. I've no time for you just now. Later, we will not be so hurried.'

He released her nose and turned away, trotting down the track. He stopped once to turn and make a gesture that she thought was a blown kiss. Then he rounded a corner of the wood and Grace was left to contemplate the view across the Firth and the horrors of her predicament.

God alone knew what was happening down at the house. Her fears for Stuart were almost overpowering but her own state was bad enough. Her mouth was totally obstructed. Her nose was beginning to run so that her craving for oxygen was becoming paramount. By twisting her neck painfully, she managed to blow her nose against the tree-trunk, but one nostril was still blocked and breathing remained a struggle.

She could neither free her hands nor reach the knot behind the tree. How long did she have before the man came back? It was the loneliest place in the world and she was the loneliest person in it. She had never seen a farmer or a forester in the area. How often did they visit? Once a month? To make bad worse, she was sitting on a sharp stone. She began to struggle to get to her feet. She managed to work the twine up with her, towards where the trunk of the tree was less thick, but she was wasting precious oxygen and she was only half-crouched when the twine caught in the bark and she had still not gained enough slack to reach the knot. She was caught between sitting and standing with nowhere to go.

How long she was stuck there, prey to many fears, to cramps in her injured muscles and to the struggle for breath, she never worked out. She came to feel that she could not bear a minute more, but more minutes dragged by. To scream might at least have relieved her feelings but her mouth was full. She tried to pinch the end of the sock between the tree and her shoulder but it was a forlorn attempt.

The first warning of more misery to come was when her ears threatened to burst into flames. It took her a second or two to recognise that the midges, well known in the entomology books as 'The Scourge of Scotland', had been attracted to the smell of her sweat in their tens of thousands. Small enough to be virtually invisible, their individual bites added up to an excruciating torture. At liberty, she would have dashed indoors, to seek cold water, insect repellent or soothing ointments. But she could neither scratch nor even brush them away. The burning spread to her forehead, her cheeks, the corners of her eyes, even her thighs and calves. A puff from one of Stuart's cigarettes might have afforded a little relief.

There was nothing to do but endure.

The first herald of rescue was a large black dog that came bounding down the track, put a cold, wet nose up her skirt, aimed a generous lick in the direction of her face and then loped away back in the direction from which it had come. Was the dog Maisie, or a stray? More time ground past while the burning in her wrists was eclipsed by the white heat in her back and thighs and the flame where the midges attacked. Then the dog re-appeared and behind it, as if on a golden chariot, fluttering his wings and to the sound of a fanfare, came Geordie Munro.

When he saw Grace, Geordie goggled but to her relief he only checked his stride for a moment. He arrived at a run. 'My God!' he said. 'My God!' He picked at the knot behind the tree and after some seconds it came free and she was able to rise to her full height and take the strain off her back and legs. She could have wept with relief, both at the lessening of the muscular torture and that the first arrival had not been a local rapist. 'Who did this to you?' he demanded. He was picking away at the knots at her hands, but the knots were between her wrists and the twine was tangled. 'If I'd only a knife,' he said.

Grace, beside herself with frustration, made a frantic noise through her nose and Geordie took hold of the sock and pulled. The sock came away without quite taking any of her teeth with it. Grace drew several deep breaths, worked a trace of moisture into her mouth and said, 'Can you get me free?'

'Dashed if I can, Lassie. We'd better go down to the houses for a knife.'

On the point of leading a dash down the hill, Grace recovered her wits and thought again. There was a patch pocket on her skirt but she could see and feel that it was empty. 'Where's my mobile phone?' she said. Had the man taken it away with him? But no, she looked towards where he had knocked her down and she could see its gleam among the dead needles. 'Quickly,' she said. 'My phone. Call the police.' She had to point with her toe. While he fetched it, she stooped and let the anxious Maisie cool her face with comforting licks.

Under her direction, Geordie managed to switch on the phone, key in the number for the emergency services and hold the phone while she was put through to the police. She gave directions to Strathmore.

'Your name and address, caller.'

'In a minute. Get help there.'

'A car is already on the way,' the Control operator said patiently. 'There was a car at Morangie and it's been directed to the scene. It's probably halfway there by now. Your name and address?'

Chastened, Grace gave her name and explained that she was temporarily resident at Strathmore. Geordie terminated the call for her and dropped the phone into her pocket.

'We must get down there,' Grace said. She turned to run but Geordie had stooped to recover her sock and trainer and he was standing on an end of the twine. She was jerked to an agonising halt. When they set off again down the hill she found it difficult to remain balanced while hurrying on the uneven surface with her hands behind her. Geordie took her arm to steady her. Puzzled, Maisie circled around them, in danger of getting under their feet. The way seemed much longer than ever before but at least they soon left most of the midges behind.

When at last they arrived at the roadside, Geordie paused. The roof of a white car showed in the driveway of Strathmore.

'Dashed if I'm crossing the road this way,' he said. 'Anyone sees, they'll think I'm abducting you. I'll go first.' He hurried across the road. Grace was almost on his heels.

The white car was, as she had supposed, a police car. Beside it, in a contorted position, lay a police constable. He was semi-conscious and bleeding from the nose. His jaw looked as though it might be broken.

Geordie managed to phone the emergency services, this time, without her help. He was flustered but she left him calling for more police assistance and an ambulance while she hurried into the house. Her wrists were still tied and she had to twist awkwardly to open the door. Her first concern was for her patient.

It was immediately obvious that the contents of the house had been turned upside down. A heavy chest, which had stood in the hall, had been overturned. Clothes had been tossed out through bedroom doors. Stuart's door was shut and after backing against it to turn the handle she tripped on a tumbled coat and fell. Without more than token use of her hands, she found it impossible to get to her feet. She was trying to roll against the wall when she found Stuart standing over her, unsteadily but undoubtedly upright. He began to pull her to her feet.

Professional concern over-rode other fears. 'Careful,' she said quickly. 'Don't load your joints.'

He finished the movement and then returned with an exaggerated limp and rolled onto the bed. 'Bring me your scissors,' he said.

She crossed to the chest of drawers and fumbled behind her back for the scissors. Her first concern was whether he had undone her handiwork. While he was cutting her free, she said, 'Do your joints hurt?'

'Not my joints, no. That wasn't exactly comfortable, but I don't think I've done any damage.'

'Thank the Lord for small mercies!' Her wrists came free. She turned and saw for the first time that there was blood on his face. 'Oh my God!' she said. 'What else happened to you?'

'It's not as bad as I think it looks. A nosebleed and a cut lip. They knew that I was no threat to them.'

'And you've got a lump like half a tennis-ball coming up on your forehead.'

'It'll go down again. Please, go and see what happened to my uncle.'

Blood was returning to her hands. The pins and needles were excruciating but it was better to be occupied. She tried the kitchen. The contents of the cupboards had been thrown around the room. She didn't see Duncan Cameron at first. Then she found him, hidden by the overturned table. One of his arms looked broken and he was either deeply unconscious or dead. She stooped and felt for a pulse in his neck.

Stuart was still spread-eagled on the bed but he turned his head as she came in. What she could see of his face looked frantic. 'Your uncle's alive,' she said, 'but he's badly hurt.' She crossed to the basin and at last had to blessing of cold water to soothe her burning skin. Despite the horrors of the situation, she could have wept with relief.

'You'd better call an ambulance.'

'There's one on its way.'

'Goddamn! I suppose this means the police will have to be involved.'

She would have laughed at him if the whole situation had not been more terrible than anything she had ever known. 'Not a lot of doubt about that. There's a damaged constable outside. I'd better go and see how he is.' She left the basin reluctantly and dried her hands and face.

'Dear Lord!' he said. He rolled his head from side to side. 'What a mess! What a hell of a mess!' She was in no doubt that he was in torment but she could not think of any comforting words to offer him.

14

The day, for Grace, became a blur. Never afterwards could she remember the sequence of events. With Geordie's help, she did what little she could to make the police constable and Mr Cameron comfortable. At the least, she made sure that each was breathing naturally. That must have been before more police arrived, including a detective sergeant from Dornoch.

An ambulance, complete with paramedics, removed Duncan Cameron and the injured constable to hospital and at least one of the other police went along in the hope of taking statements. Geordie Munro, having told what little he knew, was released to go to the dental appointment which had kept him away from his work. Grace remembered to be grateful for the infected tooth that explained his arrival to the rescue, although Geordie considered it less of a blessing. Grace seemed, in retrospect, simultaneously to be reiterating the same statement over and over, ministering to Stuart, nursing her own bruises and anointing her insect bites. The thermal pads that she had been keeping in the freezer proved their worth.

She was allowed to attend to Stuart only under the supervision of a constable, and for the remainder of her time they were segregated. She was permitted to do as much tidying as was necessary to determine that, to her limited knowledge, nothing of any significance seemed to have been removed. (She was relieved to note that though her precious equipment had been shifted around no serious damage had occurred, unlike Stuart's two computers, which had been totally vandalised.)

She was also permitted to make first lunch and then afternoon tea for herself and Stuart, although his was served to him by one or other of the police. To her relief and somewhat to her surprise, she found that arrangements had been made for the refreshment of the police and that she was not required to provide catering. The remainder of her time was spent alone in the kitchen, where she had been permitted to restore some sort of order – either leafing through Duncan Cameron's sporting magazines or staring vaguely out of the window. Somewhere beyond the jumble of disasters there might be some kind of order but her mind refused at first to make sense of it. During the intervals of solitude, she had plenty of time for unwilling thought. With the disorder of a dream, her mind threw up scenarios ranging from the credible to the fantastic, but by mid-afternoon it was working again with some semblance of logic.

The intrusion of unexplained and violent crime into a usually placid and law-abiding area was causing a stir, but if one of their own had not been assaulted she thought that the police might have been treating the event as comparatively trivial. A house had been ransacked and some damage had occurred but nothing had been stolen. A woman had been tied up but not sexually assaulted. Two men had been beaten up, but perhaps not a great deal more seriously than in your average Saturday night pub fight. The lower orders of the police were making a meal of it, hoping to impress their seniors with a triumphant piece of discovery or deduction. Grace was quite sure that there had been a great deal more behind the invasion than showed on the surface, but to introduce her suspicions in present company would have been to invite endless argument and little comprehension. In addition to which, her faith in the infallibility of the police was qualified by the thought that one of the constables attending was almost certainly the officer who had reported Stuart's fall to be accidental.

Her conversation with Jenny Welles came back to her. After some deliberation, she requested that Inspector Welles be informed that she might have some useful information for his personal ears. More than that, she refused to say. To her surprise, this was accepted after only token attempts to question her. Apparently such deviousness was not unknown and it was not considered proper for officers to interrogate each other's informants. Even so, she was quite surprised when, only an hour later, a sandy-haired young man with a broken nose walked in and introduced himself as Inspector Welles.

'You're Jenny's husband?' she said. She had been picturing somebody quite different.

'I am,' he said. He shook her hand before settling in the chair opposite. He had a surprisingly deep and pleasant voice and a slightly pedantic mode of speech. 'And you must be the physiotherapist who was making enquiries about Mr Campbell's fall. If I had to make a guess, it would be that you now fear that today's episode has occurred because you have been making progress towards a conclusion.'

'I feel rather silly, now that I hear somebody say it aloud,' she admitted.

He smiled kindly. 'Tell me the rest and I'll judge whether it's silly.'

His manner reassured her. 'This isn't the first time that I've had a patient who took a fall onto his knees and elbows,' Grace said. She had repeated the story so often that she felt it necessary to find a change of wording each time. 'These injuries didn't seem consistent with that cause. It's always important to me to know how the injuries arose, but this patient only repeats the story and pleads loss of memory. He also flatly refuses to be left alone in the house. Frankly, I think that he's been intimidated and events seem to bear that out. He hated the idea of bringing the police into it, but things have gone beyond the point at which he can keep them to himself.'

'A long way beyond,' the inspector agreed.

'I started asking a few questions and it seemed to snowball. Your wife gave me prints of the photographs she'd taken at the time. Of course, they showed dozens of faces, very few of which I had seen before, so I asked friends to put names and details to as many as they could. I'm afraid that word got around.'

Inspector Welles sat quietly for a few seconds while he considered. He leaned forward for a minute and studied the marks on her wrists. Grace felt herself begin to fidget under his calm scrutiny. Since being knocked down, tied up, dragged around and half eaten by midges, several hours earlier, she had managed to wash and to brush her hair but she was certain that she was overdue for a shower, clean clothes and access to her makeup box.

'You think that they may have been after your photographs,' he said at last. 'But you told the officers that nothing seemed to have been taken.'

Other concerns had predominated in Grace's mind for the past few days but she remembered suddenly and blessed her forgetfulness. 'The photographs aren't here,' she said. 'My car got side-swiped off the road two days ago, by a Land Rover that didn't stop. I still haven't worked out whether it was an accident or deliberate, but what's happened today makes me think that it was deliberate. My car was taken to the garage. The photographs will still be in the glove compartment. Stuart – Mr Campbell – offered me the loan of his car to go and fetch my odds and ends but I was still feeling a bit shaken and not ready yet to drive somebody else's more expensive car.'

'Excuse me for a moment.' He left the kitchen. Grace thought that he was exceptionally polite and considerate, for a policeman. Perhaps that was his technique – to lure the interviewee into a sense of false security and then to pounce. He returned and resumed his seat. 'I suppose it's possible,' he said. 'On the other hand, the information that you and your friends have accumulated must be public knowledge, so stealing the photographs wouldn't have suppressed it. I've seen them and there were no startling revelations.'

Grace had been close to arriving at the same conclusion but she was not going to allow him to dismiss her efforts so lightly. 'The combination of something in one of the photographs with some piece of local knowledge might add up to your startling revelation,' Grace pointed out. 'Would you accept that the truth may show up when you put all the right bits of public knowledge together in the right order?'

He smiled. 'That's often true. But the fact remains that the search and the violence were mostly confined to this house. Your attacker did not interrogate you as to where whatever-it-is... is,' he finished lamely. 'Which suggests that the photographs were not the objective.' He got to his feet. 'You'll have to excuse me again.'

'Is it all right if I do some more clearing up in here?' she asked.

'Go right ahead.'

She resumed her tidying of the kitchen, restoring whatever was salvable to the cupboard, consigning what was ruined to a plastic rubbish bag and trying to isolate some ingredients for an evening meal. When the Inspector returned, the room was looking almost respectable again.

He put a carrier bag on the table and they sat. 'These are your personal odds and ends from your car,' he said. 'I have the photographs. Leave them with me for a day and I'll see what I can make of them. But for now, I'd like you to come through and speak with your patient. He is adamantly refusing to say anything to the point.'

The butterflies in Grace's tummy returned along with a generation of caterpillars. 'Must I?'

'No, of course not. I can't force you. But I honestly don't think he's doing himself any favours by staying quiet. He seems to think a lot of you. The few words that he has managed to utter have mostly been enquiries about your health and safety. Perhaps you can get him to see sense.'

Humbly, Grace followed the Inspector across the hall while considering his words. Could *think a lot of you* have a double-edged meaning? The Inspector stood back to allow her to enter first. Was this more courtesy than was usually to be expected from a provincial policeman or something calculated? If the latter, it reached its presumed objective. There was something ominous about being treated kindly by a policeman.

Incongruous sunshine was flooding the garden but the room was dull after the bright kitchen. Stuart had resumed his previous position but on their entry he removed his forearm from across his eyes and half raised himself to look at Grace with the reproachful gaze of a whipped spaniel. 'This is all your fault,' he said.

Grace had an unhappy feeling that he was probably right, but she refused to accept all the blame without an argument. She set to briskly, tidying his tumbled sheets. 'You don't know that,' she said. 'Perhaps it was all going to happen anyway. I wouldn't have had to ask any questions if you'd been frank with me from the beginning. If you don't tell us what it's really all about, we can't be sure.'

Stuart half-opened his mouth and seemed about to speak. Then the dogged look came down over his face and he shook his head.

'I think you would be well advised to reconsider,' the Inspector said. 'What they were after had little or nothing to do with Miss Gillespie. The house has been thoroughly searched but there's little sign of damage except in the little room at the end of the hall, the one you seem to have been using as an office or study. If you had any disks there, they've gone.' The Inspector paused temptingly but Stuart remained still and quiet. 'And they've taken a hammer to your computers, smashing them open and removing the hard drives. Of course, if they got what they were after, this may be the end of the matter. If not... Your uncle has been seriously injured; Miss Gillespie was assaulted, threatened and tied up and you've sustained further injury. She has a point, you know. She may have triggered today's events, out of innocence and good intentions; but none of it could have happened if you'd spoken out at the time. At least give us your description of the men.'

'Please, Stuart,' Grace said. 'Anything I've done, I did because I wanted to do my best for you. Speak up now and we can put the whole thing behind us.'

Stuart was shaking his head. 'I couldn't,' he said, 'and

I still can't. God!' he burst out. 'If only you'd left well enough alone instead of meddling.'

'But was it well enough?' Grace grabbed at another thought as it flitted through her mind. 'Do you think they were the same men that threw you off the roof?'

He seemed to be on the point of answering. Then he glared and shook his head.

'All right,' Grace said. 'You didn't trust me before so you obviously won't trust me again. You're determined not to forgive me. I'd better go. I'll recommend another physio for you.'

Stuart managed to drag himself into a sitting position, making a sound of negation and despair. 'That isn't what I meant,' he said miserably. He made a grab for her hand. Grace was pleased to notice, with an independent part of her mind, that his grip was a little stronger. His attitude seemed to have undergone a *volte face*. 'Don't go,' he said. 'Please don't go. I do trust you. And I don't have to forgive you anything. You couldn't possibly have known what a hornet's nest you were stirring up. I can't say any more. But please do stay.'

'Of course I'll stay,' Grace said. She had had no intention of leaving.

'I think you're both missing a point or two,' said the Inspector. 'You can hardly stay here, out in the country. An injured patient, a woman who would be tied to the house to look after him and no certainty that the attackers won't return. I don't have the resources to mount a guard over you, twenty-four hours a day and seven days a week. Mr Campbell will have to go back into hospital, at least until he decides to open up and tell us what's at the back of this.'

'Would you come with me?' Stuart asked Grace. She thought that he was looking twenty years older and sick.

'I don't think they'd accept that. They'd have their own physiotherapists.'

'If you tell all,' the Inspector said, 'we can gather up whatever's gone adrift and you would then be safe to stay here.'

Stuart leaned back and closed his eyes, but Grace could see that, though he was near the end of his tether, he was still not ready to speak. 'Suppose I got somebody to come and stay here with us,' she suggested. As she spoke she could see a dozen reasons why that would not work. For a start, whom could she get? And, among the few faintly possibles, who could be expected to stand up to the thugs if they returned? Which of them, indeed, could be trusted to read a shopping list and return with the correct supplies. 'I have a better idea,' she said. 'Suppose I take him to my parents' house in Dornoch? Instead of being out in the wilds, there are people round about and the house isn't much more than a long stone's throw from Dornoch Police Station.'

'Would you do that?' Stuart asked. 'Could you?' The relief in his tone touched Grace's heart.

'That sound like an excellent idea,' the Inspector said. 'There would be room?'

'My room has been kept for me,' Grace said, 'and there's more than one spare. I'll check that no visitors are expected.' In the privacy of her own mind, she had already decided that the move would take place whether visitors were expected or not, even if she herself had to sleep on the floor of her father's study.

Mrs Gillespie was appalled to hear even an expurgated version of the day's upheaval, but although flustered she expressed delight at the prospect of a return of her daughter to the nest, and especially if accompanied by an eligible young man. It had been a great disappointment to the good lady that Grace's patients had so often been either elderly ladies or married footballers, the latter often with appalling records of bad behaviour. A bachelor depute headmaster, even one with a slightly spotted reputation, could only be an improvement. She embarked on an immediate orgy of sheet and towel airing before dashing to the shops.

When it came to the immediate logistics of the move, Inspector Welles proved remarkably helpful. When Grace sought assistance in adjusting Stuart's car to carry a patient with inflexible knees, he summoned a return of the ambulance. Clothes had been flung around during the original attack and further disturbed by the police in an over-zealous search for clues. The local PC, he whose investigation of Stuart's original accident was proving to have erred on the side of slapdash, was set to bundling them into cases and cartons. Grace would have preferred to deal with her own underwear but she was busy rescuing and stowing her precious equipment and ensuring that Stuart's personal necessities were included. Moreover, the young man had a roguish look and a twinkle in his eye, so it was improbable that he would be handling anything that he had not seen the like of before.

The luggage was loaded into the back and boot of

Stuart's car. When the Inspector sensed that Grace was nervous at the prospect of driving again, and in an unfamiliar car, he chauffeured her to Dornoch himself. Grace decided that this courtesy was not extended to her because she was an old friend of his boss's wife but simply out of good nature. As they moved off, she looked back at Strathmore almost nostalgically. The bungalow had begun to seem like home. The Inspector carried the heavier items into the house before returning to Strathmore as a passenger in a traffic car. He would come back the next day, he said, and Geordie Munro's sister, who obliged with the cleaning of Strathmore whenever Duncan Cameron's back was playing him up, had already been given the keys and asked to straighten the house as soon as the police had vacated it.

The ambulance arrived before the traffic car was out of sight. Stuart was conveyed by the ambulance men to a spare room. Grace had considered offering to exchange rooms, because her old bedroom was slightly the larger, had the better view and already contained a television, but the best spare room was on the ground floor and convenient to the kitchen, one bathroom and the outside world. The room had once been the province of Grace's older sister, now married to a farmer in Northumberland and blissfully contented with a life devoted to domesticity and children. Grace could only hope that Stuart would soon accept but not wish to emulate the pastel colours and frills. Another advantage of the room was that her sister had been a smoker, so it would not suffer any additional contamination.

Grace had phoned the hospital and had been assured that Duncan Cameron, although still unconscious and found to have several broken ribs, was stable. The injured constable was doing as well as could be expected. She passed this news to Stuart as soon as he was settled in bed. He received it in a silence that lasted through the evening meal provided by Mrs Gillespie.

He was still very quiet when she resumed his treatment in their new quarters. She worked in silence for a few minutes, moving his limbs to mobilise the joints while he remained passive. His hips seemed to be none the worse for his having risen prematurely to his feet when she needed his help, but there was an unfamiliar tension in his muscles. If he were going to indulge in an extended sulk while he was a guest in her parents' house, life would become impossible.

'I'm not forgiven then?' she suggested.

She felt him jump. 'I'm sorry,' he said. 'There's nothing to forgive. My mind was miles away. I've been... ungracious. And after you've brought me into your home.' He sighed deeply. 'Coals of fire, coals of fire.'

'Rubbish!' she said. 'Perhaps I did bring these troubles on us. But perhaps I didn't. Had you considered that?'

'I'm still considering it and I don't know what to think. Maybe I don't want to know. People,' he said petulantly, 'are always fretting about causes when it's effects that matter. And now the effect is that we've got the police sniffing around.' He sighed. 'I don't know what's going to be the end of it all. And I don't know what to do except hold my tongue and hope for the best. And I mean hold my tongue, so don't press me, because I'm not going to say any more than that. I don't expect you to shoulder my burdens.'

Grace wanted to say that she would be happy to share his burdens. She would have liked to point out that she had been sharing them for some days. But it was too soon and the mood was wrong. 'But why does it matter?' she asked.

He shook his head. 'If you knew that, you'd know it all,' he retorted.

There was still that unnatural muscular tension, while his voice and expression underlined his anxiety. Grace would have liked to make another attempt to coax him into opening up, but it seemed to her that his only reason for refusing to seek the help and protection of the police was that he himself had been doing something disreputable, if not downright criminal. In that event, would she betray him to the forces of the Law? That might depend on just how wicked he had been but, looking at him with freshly opened eyes, she was sure that whatever he had been doing could not be so very heinous. Whenever she tried to imagine him being sneaky or evil or committing any sin beyond forgivable naughtiness, she found that some other face had become attached to the sinner. It had taken her only a few days to get the measure of him. She had met the type before, a man skilled and intelligent in his own speciality and therefore one with glowing prospects, but sadly lacking in worldly wisdom and common sense. A man, in fact, who needed the support and guidance of a strong-minded woman. The world was full of them both, and winning combinations they made.

It was time to leave that subject for the moment and to consider, in the privacy of her mind, whether she should be less forthcoming with the police until she knew more. She had finished his treatment. She sat down in a spindly bedside chair and tried to relax. 'You've been missing your treats,' she said.

His expression lightened immediately. 'I haven't, you know,' he said. 'You left two cans of expensive beer in

156

the bedside cabinet. I gave one to a constable in exchange for a handful of cigarettes.'

She chuckled. 'The old Highland talent for barter,' she commented. Her mood dipped again. 'I don't know your uncle well enough for hospital visiting and you're certainly not able. When he comes round, will he get any visitors? I don't like to think of him lying there and feeling neglected. Moral support is important for recovery.'

He reached out and took her hand. 'You're very generous, considering how he spoke to you. But don't worry about him. He's in several clubs and the members of at least one of them make a point of visiting the sick.'

With relief, Grace stopped thinking about Duncan Cameron. She had enough worries without him.

Later, she was returning from the utility room, where she had been ironing some of the wrinkles out of their crumpled clothes, when she met her mother in the hall. Mrs Gillespie was trying to hide something behind a bottom that was well designed for hiding things, but Grace had been alert for any embarrassing activity on her mother's part. She made a grab and got hold of an early family album.

'Mother,' she said in tones of reproach. 'How could you?'

Mrs Gillespie looked defiant. 'Well, he was asking all about you and when I said that we had some snaps of you as a child he asked me. He insisted. He did, really.'

Grace returned the album. 'You will oblige me by putting it away in the bottom of the darkest cupboard and never, ever taking it out again.'

Her mother promised, but Grace could tell that she was insincere.

Stuart was looking pleased. 'Now I've seen you topless,' he said.

'On the beach, aged four.'

'You were a beautiful baby.'

'What a pity that I had to grow up!'

'Never say that,' Stuart said earnestly. 'You grew into a beautiful woman. I never get over marvelling that you look so... stately, and yet inside you there's a warm and vital person with a real sense of humour.'

Grace had never been called stately before. She would have liked to have pursued the topic a little further but instead she said, 'So now you've seen all my baby photographs. When do I get to see yours?'

'Never. I was a hideous baby. Yes, I've seen you on roller skates and also dressed as a fairy. The one I liked best,' he said, 'was the shot of you with the telephone in your hands, looking so serious and businesslike.'

Grace found herself laughing. 'I was only three. Did my mother tell you what had happened when that one was taken? No? The police had come round to the house because several nine-nine-nine calls had come from our number without anybody speaking.'

'And that was you?'

'That was me.' Grace remembered that she was speaking to a depute headmaster. 'That was indeed I. There was no significance for me in the number. The nine, being at the bottom right-hand corner, happened to be the most accessible for a right-handed child. Perhaps that's why the Americans use nine-one-one instead.'

'I've asked your mother to look out the negative,' Stuart said.

Grace had become accustomed to adjusting quickly to unfamiliar beds. But a return to her own bed, combining

158

the strange with the familiar, proved oddly unsettling. Added to the events of the day, it made sleep evasive. She lay, progressing in and out of dozing sleep, while her mind toyed with the questions surrounding Stuart. Why was a naturally open person being so secretive? Her acquaintance with him had been as much through the senses conveyed by her fingertips as through his looks and words, but her every attempt to picture him as a villain still failed. Maddeningly, and pushing sleep further beyond reach, was the certainly that somewhere in her last exchanges with Stuart was tucked away a vital clue. Or was it perhaps only the association with photographs?

She dozed again and awoke with a fresh thought in her mind. There was a possibility, and a good one, that Stuart could have a good reason to keep his own counsel and still be... no, not virtuous. Not moral. But ethical. He could be protecting somebody else and, as her sleepy mind filled in the details, she could see only one scenario. He was protecting a lady's good name. He had been pushed off the roof by a jealous husband or lover.

That, to Grace made perfect sense. In the days when she had been working on his body she had become increasing aware of his attractiveness as a man. She had tried not to notice it, but there was no doubt in her mind that he exuded sexuality. She could hardly have been unaware that his virility was easily aroused. How could any woman not fall for his charms and set her cap at him? And who could blame a man of his vigour for falling for the charms of such a siren as Elaine? This conclusion, far from tainting his image, added more than a touch of romantic gallantry.

She fell asleep at once and when she awoke she was aware of having dreamed. She could not remember her dreams, but she knew that they had been somehow special. She tried to return to sleep to recapture the golden images but they had escaped forever. Her reasoning, however, was still clear in her mind. There was, of course, the possibility that he was protecting a friend who had sinned in some other way, but the theory of a romantic entanglement seemed somehow so right that it had taken over the centre of the stage. Douglas Burrard, the former boyfriend of Elaine and now believed to be back in favour, was the obvious contender. He was, after all, the only suspect who had in actuality gained something from it. Whether what he had gained would prove worth the effort remained to be seen. Grace had her own opinion about that.

As she gave Stuart his morning treatment she was increasingly aware of a magic spark in each physical contact. It was as faint and yet perfect as the scent from the flower on a vine, so beloved by Francis Bacon.

16

Stuart's mood had settled into one of passive acceptance. Whatever the future might bring, he would await it uncomplainingly. Grace had brought the television set from her own bedroom. Previously, he had complained bitterly at the 'dumbing-down' of the programmes. Chasing cheap ratings, he said, resulted in encouraging the ignorant to lower their standards ever further. But now he lay, watching the daytime rubbish without taking in a word, not even to criticise the manifold errors in fact and syntax. Despite his words of the previous evening, she remained unsure whether he had really forgiven her for bringing the police about his ears. For reassurance, she kept trying to recall the warmth in his voice.

When she had done what she could for his health and hygiene without eliciting a word of either thanks or reproach, she decided that there was no point in offering company to somebody who seemed unaware of her presence and he might as well be left to his own devices. Nothing had been heard from the police, so she felt free to go for a fast jog around the golf courses.

She came back feeling less stressed but in need of a quick shower. The mobile phone caught her in the act. She wrapped herself in her towel and retrieved the phone from the top of the toilet cistern.

The caller was Derek McTaggart. 'You asked about Dean Murray,' he said. 'One of my bar staff knows his mother. His father has a Land Rover.'

'You wouldn't know if it's had a dent in the rear near-side corner?'

'No, I wouldn't.'

'Could you take a look, next time he calls in at the bar?'

'He's banned from here. But don't tell him that I told you *anything* about him. He isn't a man I'd want to quarrel with.'

'You managed to ban him without quarrelling?'

'I didn't ban him. It was the police, through the sheriff.'

'Don't worry about it,' she said. 'Thanks anyway.' She was cold and still soapy. She got back under the shower.

There was still no word from the police. When she was dressed, she decided to take a leisurely walk down to the shops. Stuart's car was taking up space outside her father's garage but she had still not nerved herself to drive it in traffic. Her route was so familiar that within a few paces it was as if she had never been away. As she neared the heart of Dornoch the red stone police station, looking more like a block of flats than a shrine to public order, loomed up. She found herself trying to avoid eye contact with it. She felt guilty by association, without the satisfaction of knowing association with what...

Her own minor errands, including some dietary requirements for Stuart, were soon accomplished. On an afterthought, it occurred to her that Stuart would be very short of his 'treats'. He would be unable to purchase them for himself and might feel inhibited by any remaining tension between them from asking her to provide him with luxuries of which he knew that she disapproved. A peace offering might be due. She added a six-pack of beer and several packets of cigarettes to her shopping and set off back up the hill on foot, struggling against the increased weight in her basket.

She was saved the burden of carrying her load all the way home. She had only progressed a little past the police station when Inspector Welles pulled up in an unmarked Ford. The Inspector and another man got out and Grace was ushered into the front passenger seat. The Inspector resumed the wheel while the other man managed to fold his considerable length into the back. Her initial fear that she was being invited into the police station to help the police with their enquiries proved unfounded, but the Inspector did make a polite request for a word with her at her home. She returned to her former home in some comfort.

The dining room, a large room with a view over the sunlit garden, was available for conference. They settled in mahogany chairs around the highly polished table. Mrs Gillespie furnished them, unasked, with coffee, promised to see to any needs of Stuart's and left them to it. The tall man was introduced as Tom Ballintore, the local Detective Sergeant.

'We've had a good look through your photographs without being much further forward,' the Inspector said. 'Have you managed to persuade Mr Campbell to recover his memory?'

'I'm afraid not. I'm still working on it.'

'Sergeant Ballintore will be conducting the investigation locally. Before he starts his enquiries, he would be helped if you'd tell him what you make of my wife's photographs.'

The Sergeant put his elbows on the table and then, apparently with some confused recollection of table manners, removed them again. In addition to being tall, he was thin with a lined, sad face under sparse grey-brown hair. 'At first glance,' he said, 'it might seem like we have two or three isolated occurrences. Mr Campbell could have fallen and your car been rammed in two coincidental accidents. But take those together with the attacks on yourself, Constable Beattie, Mr Campbell and Mr Cameron and it may be that you were right and the local constable was wrong. Please tell us if you have gained any more from your... investigations.' The police habitually resent any attempt by the public to carry out criminal investigations on their own behalves and the Sergeant's face made it clear that he felt guilty of uttering a dirty word.

Grace found that her feelings were becoming scrambled. What she had so far assembled seemed very thin. If it turned out to have no substance, Stuart would presumably be in the clear. But as the Sergeant implied, surely so many coincidences would stretch the laws of probability.

'It started because Mr Campbell's injuries didn't match up with the idea that he just plain fell off the roof,' she said. 'If he'd come down on his knees and elbows, his hips and shoulders would certainly have been damaged. In addition, the bruises on his back remained unexplained. I started asking questions and looking at Mrs Welles's photographs and I found that Mr Campbell, who seems to be a totally inoffensive person, has made some enemies.'

'But how many of those enemies appear in the photographs?' the Sergeant asked quickly.

'They don't have to be in the photographs,' Grace pointed out. 'For instance, Mr Campbell has been arguing against the contractor being allowed to negotiate a further contract instead of having to tender again for it. I don't know a lot about contracting but, as I understand it, the profit would be reduced and they might not even get the continuation contract. Any of the contractor's men could have felt that his job was at risk and have caught Mr Campbell on his way down the stairs. And, of course, Land Rovers are ten a penny in the construction industry.'

Grace had begun with a feeling that she was in front of her old headmistress again, but now she was regaining her courage. As she spoke, her facts seemed to be marshalling themselves. 'In the photographs,' she said, 'you can see a man known as Dougie – Douglas, I suppose – Burrard, who works for the contractor.' She pointed out the slightly corpulent figure in one of the photographs.

The Sergeant looked at her blandly, registering neither acceptance nor disbelief. 'You're suggesting that he might have been the attacker for the sake of his employer's profitability?'

'It isn't as silly as you make it sound. Such things have happened. But he had another motive. Until recently Mr Campbell had a girlfriend called Elaine something – I never heard her last name. Her previous boyfriend was the same Mr Burrard and I gather that there was some aggravation when she transferred her affections to Mr Campbell. She has now transferred them back, not wanting to tie herself to a man who, she thinks, might never be fully active again. You'll note that Mr Burrard doesn't seem to be in any of the frames around the time of Mr Campbell's fall, yet I'm told that he was present to work the hoist when the stretcher was lowered to the ambulance.'

The Sergeant registered interest. Evidently, for some reason of his own, he found sexual jealousy a more credible motive than a mere wish to remain in employment instead of enjoying the benefits of the Welfare State. 'Anyone else?'

'I think so. The contractor asked the school for a few senior pupils, to take round trays of drinks and canapés. One of them, Dean Murray – this one – had been suspended for a while because of a row with Mr Campbell. He was sent home again two days ago for a prank at school. His father has a Land Rover.'

'Where was he just before Mr Campbell fell?' the Sergeant asked.

After a hunt through the stack of photographs, Grace isolated two prints and turned them for the Sergeant's inspection. 'Just before the fall, the boy seems to be mooching to the left, out of the camera's view.'

'Away from Mr Campbell and the stairs?'

'True, though that doesn't mean that he didn't cross the roof again without being caught by the camera. He might even have gone round behind the photographer. But in the photographs he seems to be heading towards the other corner of the roof, a corner which appears in one of the earlier photographs.' Grace hunted again through the pile. The shot that she wanted had got out of sequence and she had a momentary fear that it had been lost, but her eye lit on it at last. 'This one. You'll see that the rope handrail begins and ends at that corner; and from there I think that one could see the place from which Stuart – Mr Campbell – fell. It might have started as no more than another prank, but if Mr Campbell leaned against the rope to look down onto the roof below and somebody suddenly slacked off the rope, perhaps intending no more than to give him a fright...'

The Sergeant looked at the photograph without enthusiasm. 'How do you suggest young Murray knew that Mr Campbell was going to lean against the rope and look down from that place?'

'I don't suggest any such thing,' Grace said. The

Sergeant was only doing his job but he was beginning to irritate her. 'It's possible that Dean Murray withdrew to the corner of the roof, to have a surreptitious smoke or something, and then saw Mr Campbell arrive at the other corner and look down. And he saw his chance to give his enemy a fright. When Mr Campbell really did fall, he'd have felt guilty and vulnerable and then, when I started asking questions, he would have wanted to cover his tracks.'

The Sergeant sat silent, apparently stunned by the sudden rush of suspects. Inspector Welles leaned forward. 'Of course,' he said, 'you had the benefit of my wife's photographs to work from and I suspect that locals will talk to you when they won't for a policeman. All the same, strictly between ourselves, the enquiry into Mr Campbell's fall should never have been left to the local constable and, having had it dumped on him, I can think of a dozen questions he left unasked. But that's for us to worry about, not for you. Just tell me one thing. Do any of those theories – because theories are all that they are – satisfy you?'

'Not by a mile,' Grace said.

'I thought not. But it's our business to sift the facts until we find the truth. You've given us some starting points. I congratulate you.'

'I'll give you another starting point,' Grace told him. 'Has anybody checked that the Morrison brothers are still in prison? Mr Campbell gave evidence –'

'I remember the case,' the Inspector said. 'They were each turned down for parole only a week ago. And you have still got nowhere towards persuading Mr Campbell to recover his memory?'

'Nowhere at all,' Grace said. 'He's seems to have stopped blaming me for stirring things up, but that's as far as I've got. He still insists that he has no memory from that time. You can believe that or not, just as you wish.'

'But you don't believe it,' said the Inspector.

'What I believe or don't believe is of no importance and never was. I've no more to go on than you have. Loss of memory is a very difficult thing to prove, either way. I had a case like that once before, a car accident victim. I had difficulty believing him, but he turned out to be absolutely truthful. Mr Campbell seems to have lapsed into a passive state of waiting to see what you and fate can throw at him and preparing to endure it.'

Inspector Welles was nodding. 'I've seen it a hundred times. Those are often the most difficult ones to open up. We'll go and see him now. We may call for you if we think you can help.'

'All right. But he's still my patient,' Grace said. 'His state of mind is still important to his recovery.'

'We won't bully him,' said the Inspector. 'We'll start by telling him that you're within call in case he gets nervous.'

Grace set about some mundane tasks but her mind was not on them. She had loaded some of her own dirty laundry along with Stuart's pyjamas – wondering absently whether her mother would consider the juxtaposition quite proper – when Detective Sergeant Ballintore appeared suddenly at her elbow, making her jump.

'Come through, please, Miss?'

'Yes, of course.'

'You may be able to get him to open up. We certainly can't.'

Stuart was lying on his back with the TV remote control gripped firmly as if for comfort. The TV was registering an all-female talk show but in silence.

Detective Inspector Welles nodded to her and then turned back towards the bed. 'I'll ask you again, Mr Campbell. We do not believe that your memory is impaired. What caused you to fall from the roof?'

Stuart clenched his jaw but then glanced at Grace and, as if anxious not to worsen her opinion of him, said, 'I can't help what you believe or don't believe. I've had a bang on the head and I don't remember anything about it. I can't help you at all.'

Grace took a seat on the side of the bed. As if by accident, she let her hand rest against his arm. Even through his pyjama sleeve she could feel that exchange of awareness. 'Stuart,' she said, 'I'm sure that you haven't done anything wrong. You're protecting somebody else, aren't you?'

She sensed surprise in the room, from all three men. Stuart said, 'No.'

'Yes you are.' Certainty came rushing at her. 'And it's a woman. Is it Elaine? Does she have a husband? Did he push you off the roof? Are you protecting her reputation?'

Stuart looked at her for a moment in amazement. He smiled. He began to chuckle and then he was throwing himself around in the bed in the grip of convulsive laughter, so violently that Grace began to fear for his damaged joints. Some people become undignified when they laugh, exposing their worst features, but Stuart seemed to be illuminated with an inner joy. Grace felt indignation at first but his laughter was infectious and she was relieved to see him carefree if only for a minute. Soon she joined in.

'Perhaps you're not that much of a gentleman,' she said at last, which set them off again.

When they had sobered, Stuart said, 'I am quite that

much of a gentleman and more, but it didn't happen. Elaine doesn't have a husband and I have never been involved with a married woman.'

'I think I'm glad,' Grace said.

The two policemen left the room in disgust. The Inspector paused in the doorway. 'We'll come back later,' he said, 'when you may have decided that it's in your interests to be frank with us.'

17

For the rest of that week, Grace might well have thought that the police had filed the case away with other unsolved crimes. She had a single visit from Detective Sergeant Ballintore, wishing to know whether she could identify the back of a slightly out-of-focus head in one of Jenny Welles's photographs. She told him that she doubted whether even the subject's mother could make a positive identification from that image but that he almost certainly figured again in a dozen other shots. The Sergeant gave her a look suggesting that she could have helped if she had really wanted to and took the photographs away with him again.

She had plenty to occupy her without trying to duplicate the efforts of the police. Stuart was making such good progress that she was no longer afraid of overextending him. Only the slowness of the return of sensation and dexterity to his hands gave her cause for concern and also prevented him making use of the zimmer frame. She promised him that time would, as usual, be the great healer. Meantime, however, he remained dependant on her for many little personal services.

He seemed to be overcoming his worries at last. He was becoming cheerful, at times jovial, and often she felt that he was more carefree than she was. She put this down to a belief on his part that whatever he had felt to be lying in wait for him was so deeply buried that the police were not going to happen on it – either that, or his mood stemmed from the new-found freedom to indulge his little vices openly. Even when he needed none of her attention she sometimes kept him company and they laughed together or tackled the newspaper crossword. As she settled back into her old home, Grace's thoughts of violence and threats receded into the vaguest recesses of her memory and she was beginning to go confidently out and about without expecting an assailant behind every tree. She renewed her acquaintance with people and places that had figured in her youth.

Of Stuart's uncle, the news was mixed. His recovery was slow but, the hospital assured Grace, he was not short of visits from members of his various clubs. She made sure that he was well supplied with soft drinks and other comforts, but she suspected that such messages of thanks as she received had originated with the messengers.

The peaceful routine was broken when, just after Sunday lunch, she received a short and rather guarded phone call from Derek McTaggart, suggesting that she pay the hotel an immediate visit. Her first reaction was irritation that the call had come too late to save her from the heavy lunch that her mother had forced on her. However, her patient had been fed and exercised and her father had promised to keep an eye out and to telephone the police if any suspicious strangers were seen lurking in the vicinity. She had recovered sufficient confidence to tackle the use of Stuart's car. The traffic in Castle High Street gave her some anxious moments, but it took only the few miles of open road to the hotel to satisfy her that one car was really very like another, once you got used to the transposition of traffic signals and wiper control and a different feel to the clutch and steering.

After several days of mist and a cool sea breeze, the fine weather had returned. The hotel car park was again full. Derek came out to meet Grace as she left the car. As he led her through the main doors he enquired politely after her wellbeing. Grace could still feel slight after-effects from the attack on her but she assured Derek that she was recovering rapidly.

'Good, good.' Derek paused in the hall. 'I suppose you had to bring the police in after you were attacked?'

'Yes. How did you know?'

'That you were attacked? I explained once before and it's been the talk of the bars ever since. Or that you brought the police in? If that Detective Sergeant hadn't been in and out of here daily – why do people always use this place for an alibi? – there's been plenty of talk about who he's been interviewing and what about.'

'And I suppose my name's mud?'

'Not really. We usually prefer to sort out our own problems with as little recourse to the police as possible, but that's exactly what you were doing and must have been the reason you were attacked. That seems to be generally recognised and gains you some unspoken sympathy. But this isn't why I asked you to come.

'Councillor Allnith had lunch here with some men,' Derek told her. He took her elbow and guided her through the hall. 'They were talking about the attack on you and Stuart Campbell's fall and whether the two things were connected. The Councillor wanted to meet you but he didn't want to be seen going to your house or to the police. As he says, in his position he has to be everybody's friend. He has some information which could be of use to you or to the police. I can't afford to make powerful enemies either, so when he asked me to arrange a meeting I picked up the phone.'

Grace slowed her pace. 'He only wants to tell me something?'

'That's how I understand it.'

'And it will just be the two of us?'

Derek smiled 'Yes. If you're worried about being left alone with him, he doesn't have a reputation for molesting young women.'

Grace had been more concerned at the idea of there being a witness to any possible indiscretions on her part, but if the Councillor was only going to give out information she could relax. She allowed herself to be led into a parlour that was used for small parties during the winter but, being rather dark and close, was generally disused in the finer weather. Derek, after making sure that no further drinks were required, left them to themselves.

Councillor Allnith was waiting with apparent patience, a balloon glass containing half an inch of amber liquid at his elbow. As his photograph had suggested, he was thin with a pointed face that could have suggested a rodent, but he made a favourable impression by struggling to his feet out of a deep armchair and shaking her hand. Evidently old-fashioned courtesy was part of his stock-in-trade. He also produced a smile that reminded Grace that several other men of similar cast of features had proved to be perfectly affable, although some, of course, had not.

When he was quite sure that Grace was seated comfortably, he said, 'I understand that you were attacked, earlier in the week.'

'That's so.'

He tutted and shook his head disapprovingly. 'That's bad. We don't like that sort of behaviour around here. I must speak to the Police Committee. But you're recovered?'

His manner was solicitous so that Grace, although she had made up her mind to disgorge no information at all, felt that she could release at least a health bulletin. 'I'm fine,' she said. 'And Stuart Campbell was hardly touched. His uncle and the policeman are still in hospital.'

The Councillor nodded. 'I'm glad that you didn't suffer any permanent damage. Do the police suppose that the incident was connected with the questions you've been asking about the tumble that young Mr Campbell took off the school extension roof?'

'I don't know what they think,' Grace said.

'What do you think?'

Grace decided that her thoughts were her own. 'I would be guessing,' she said.

'That's true. You're very sensible. However, I suggest that their minds are bound to be working in that direction. Miss Gillespie, I have some information that might help the police with their enquiries – to coin a phrase,' he added whimsically. 'But it would not suit my purpose one bit to have it generally known that I was – um – snitching. If I confide it to you, could I count on you to pass it on to the police without revealing where it came from?' When Grace hesitated, he went on, 'Or at least to insist that they protect my identity as the source of the information?'

'I could ask them.'

The Councillor accepted the qualified assurance with a readiness that she found surprising. 'That's good. I'm sure that I can trust your discretion, and theirs. It concerns young Duncan Macrae. As you know, I was at the topping-out ceremony and so was Macrae. You probably know that Macrae is a structural engineer. At the moment, he's employed by Firth Contractors but he's desperate to go into practice for himself. You'll also be aware that I'm involved in the Leisure Complex project?'

'I understand that you're the prime mover.'

The Councillor looked less than gratified. 'You could put it like that. The offer of shares closes next week and it looks like being fully subscribed. The next step will be to take it from the stage of sketches to detailed design work. I want Macrae to take on the engineering design. It would be a big step forward for him, a chance to open his own office. So you'll see why I don't want to appear as his accuser. On the other hand, to appoint him to the Leisure Complex team and then to have him taken out of circulation would be to incur delay and substantial costs. If there were any risk of that happening, we would have to replace him with the same results. So it would suit my book to have any question of his possible guilt settled one way or the other as soon as possible. You follow me?'

Grace said that she quite understood. 'What about him?'

The Councillor beamed at her. 'That's what I like, a young lady who gets straight to the point. What you may not know is that the excavations and foundations for the school extension went a long way over budget. Well, that happens. As Macrae explained it, you can spend more money on trial holes and borings than you could possibly save. The best that can economically be done is to dig or drill a pattern of holes, make sense of the results and include for a reasonable amount of rock cutting where required or piling at soft spots. If they present a false picture, that doesn't usually affect the final cost which was always predestined. This time, one of the trial holes went down an old well in solid granite without touching the sides, right where the new boiler room was to be sunk and too close to the old school to permit blasting. The whole project was delayed several months while the compressors drilled out the granite. Macrae was called in front of the Project Committee to explain the delay and the extra cost. The other committee members were satisfied but Campbell suspected all sorts of chicanery and kickbacks and said so very loudly. He made a lot of trouble for Macrae with his employer and I know that there were bad feelings.

'I'm not saying that he gave Campbell a push, but I noticed that he seemed to have disappeared from the throng at about the same time as Campbell did. You've been studying the photographs. I had a look at the proof copies myself, to see if there were any shots that I could make use of. If you look at the first photograph after Campbell stops showing up –'

This was useful information, but Grace found something distasteful in the relish with which the Councillor was airing the engineer's possibly grubby linen. 'Would that be the one in which you're scratching your ear with one hand and your bottom with the other?' she suggested.

The Councillor was quite unfazed. 'That's the one,' he said cheerfully. 'You'll see that Macrae also seems to have vanished at about that time. I don't remember him being around after Campbell had his fall.'

'It doesn't exactly prove anything,' Grace said.

'No, of course not. But finding proof is the business of the police. They have to be given some idea of where to look. That's all that I'm suggesting. A little poking and prying and it should settle itself one way or the other.'

'If it becomes obvious that the police know about Mr Macrae's position,' she said, 'surely it will be equally obvious where the information originated.'

The Councillor looked put out. 'Not necessarily,' he said.

'The information could have reached them piecemeal from several sources.'

Councillor Allnith seemed to have said all that he had to say. When she had first got her hands on the photographs, Grace had studied them until she could have gone on *Mastermind* with their contents as her Special Subject. Stuart Campbell and Duncan Macrae were certainly seen speaking together in one frame and neither appeared to be enjoying the discussion – but that, she reminded herself, could be the normal expressions of men finding themselves forced to make conversation with somebody with whom they had no interest in common.

'I'll do the best I can,' she said. The statement could have meant anything but the Councillor thanked her warmly.

As she drove home, she wondered how it came about that the Councillor had noticed Duncan Macrae's disappearance from the photographs when his study of the proof copies had surely been before any doubts about Stuart's accident had been raised. But that question, of course, assumed that the proof prints had not been retained for his examination at a later date. The day was Sunday and the holiday traffic on the main road, heading towards John O'Groats, was heavy. She brought her mind back to her driving.

Once home she phoned the police station. Detective Sergeant Ballintore was available even late on Sunday afternoon. She passed on the suggestions. To her surprise, the Sergeant immediately accepted her request that the informant remain anonymous. Either such evasions happened regularly or perhaps he had already been in possession of the Councillor's information from other sources.

She awoke that night with a fresh thought in mind. Directing suspicion towards one person might be intended to distract it from another. Perhaps the Sergeant had not believed the Councillor. Or perhaps he had disbelieved her. She gave serious consideration to herself as a suspect but decided that she had to be above suspicion. She had been in Edinburgh when Stuart fell and she could prove it – if asked.

18

Grace was perturbed and yet perversely pleased that her relationship with her patient was moving towards a new level. The pattern was not unfamiliar. She was quite accustomed to exchanges of sexual recognition. She was, after all, female, attractive, still close to her sexual peak and not unaware of the pleasure of male attention. She had looked after herself. She was tall but her figure was good, tight waisted, generously and firmly breasted. Her hair, pale brown verging on dark blonde, was usually tightly constrained but it had a gloss and a natural wave. Her eyes were large and bright and her lips were full. It was only to be expected that the men benefiting from her skilled touch would respond with flirtation, attempts at seduction or even sincere (at the time) protestations of eternal love.

Through all these various assaults on her heart and virtue, Grace had remained aloof. Quite apart from professional proprieties, the sort of young men who came under her care were rarely men of refinement. It was true that there had been one skier, a man of great charm and not a little wealth, who had almost tempted her off the straight and narrow piste; but most of them had been wrestlers or footballers or the like, injured during the process of professional sport. They were men whose physique and skill had pulled them up out of the ruck and, while she might have considered a brief and careful affair with such masculinity and affluence outside of her professional sphere, no longer-term relationship would have been conceivable.

With Stuart, it was very different. She had been aware

from the first of his physical attractiveness. Time had shown that they shared the same tastes in books and music. They laughed freely together. Each was considerate of the other's comfort and feelings. Above all, Grace was soon sure that Stuart's physical response was to her as an individual rather than as an attractive representative of the female sex. His glances were less significant than the averting of his eyes. She had long been aware of the quick arousal of the male and Stuart's attempts to conceal both his occasional erections and his embarrassment at their occurrence attracted her sympathy. In short, they had both a strong liking and an equally strong sexual attraction. Throw in the act of sex, she thought, and you had the recipe and ingredients for love. The proof might be in the cooking. Only the ethics of her profession might prove a stumbling-block.

She had learned how cruelly a vigorous man could be tormented by unrequited lust. Several of her male patients had been outspoken on the subject. In order to spare him, she used very little makeup and no perfume other than her favourite soap. She looked out her lowest heels and her looser clothes with modest neck and hemlines and tied her hair back ever more tightly, all to little effect. The magic spark was never far away.

Instead of climaxing in an explosion, the tension between them began to resolve slowly, gently, without embarrassment on his third day in Grace's home.

There could be no doubt about his arousal. His breathing had quickened and his skin was responding to her touch. He rolled onto his side, away from her. 'I'm sorry,' he said. 'Perhaps you should defer my treatment for a while. I really am sorry.'

She went to the window and looked out. 'No need to apologise,' she said. 'I've seen it all before. It's natural.

Only an unusual woman would be insulted at being desired.'

'How very sensible!' In the silence before he spoke again, Grace could sense relief that the subject was in the open at last. Stuart cleared his throat. 'It really is you in particular,' he explained. 'Not just any woman.'

'I know.'

'It's not just that I like you a lot. It's more than liking. You're delectable. You're not girly and yet I can't get your hips out of my mind.' He chuckled. 'Usually, one can't remember such things, but when we're apart I can recall every delicious bump and hollow. My God! I'm getting excited, just thinking about them.'

She said, 'I don't think you should be talking like this.' She wanted him to go on. For a moment she was tempted to say how easily she could have responded but the time was not ripe.

'No, of course I shouldn't.'

'I can't be much help, not while you're my patient. It would be unethical.'

There was silence behind her back. Evidently he was thinking rather than sulking. 'I wouldn't expect it. How long before you can fit me into a car?'

The sudden change of subject confused her. 'Why?'

'So that I can take you out to dinner.'

She felt a wave of delight warming her inner being. So perfect, so conventional. The ancient mating ritual. The bird of prey dropping food for his mate to grab in mid-air. The animal bringing food to the den. The male feeding the female. The provider proving his ability. A date. The first step along the proper mating road.

'Your left knee still doesn't bend enough. It isn't so much the sitting in the car, it's the getting in and out. A week, perhaps two.' She hesitated. What she was about to say was not usually spoken aloud, but they had a bond, he could take it. 'Can't you give yourself some relief? I would understand.'

He held up his hands while meeting her eye. 'You've given me back some movement but I still have very little feeling. It just wouldn't work.'

She breathed a secret sigh of relief. The forbidden topic was out in the open. She was tempted to offer him relief but she decided to stick to her principles for the moment, more or less. She provided him with paper towels. Her vibrating massager would have been harmful to recent fractures and had remained unused in her baggage. She brought it out and plugged it in for him. Then she kissed him gently on the lips and left the room, but she found an excuse to loiter in the hall in case her mother should take it into her head to pay Stuart a sudden visit.

An hour later, she was in Dornoch and engaged in some minor shopping for her mother when a stocky figure rose out of a low, sporty saloon and almost bumped into her. The dark, curly hair and eyebrows above a prominent nose struck an immediate chord in her memory. She hoped to slip by unrecognised but he checked, nose to nose with her. 'It's Grace Gillespie, isn't it? You came to the Academy the year before I left.'

'And you're Duncan Macrae.'

He smiled with deliberate charm. 'I won't flatter myself by thinking that you remember my manly charms from our schooldays,' he said.

Grace decided that he needed taking down a peg or two. 'You're quite right not to,' she said. 'I'd forgotten ever having known you until this moment.'

The smile flickered but remained lit. 'I hear that you've

been poring over the photographs of the topping-out ceremony.'

There seemed to be no point in attempting to deny it, but Grace wished that people would mind their own damn businesses. 'I had a good look through them,' she admitted.

'And that's how you knew my name?' He hesitated, glancing around. 'Come for a coffee?' he suggested.

His intentions seemed peaceful. 'Why not?'

They crossed the lawn outside the cathedral under the many small trees. Coffee was served to them in the garden behind the Castle Hotel. There was a haze over the sun but the breeze had dropped and the day was balmy.

When they were alone, he said, 'I've had a damn good look at those photographs too. I've just spent more than an hour in the police station, explaining myself.' Grace was about to speak but he raised his hand. 'It's all right,' he said pacifically. 'You had to do what you thought was in the best interests of Stuart Campbell, your patient, and I never laid a finger on him; so I'm happy to get any suspicions out of the way. The Sergeant let the word "She" slip, so I guessed the information had been passed through you. And I can guess who passed it to you.'

'My lips are sealed,' Grace said lightly. 'But who do you think snitched on you?'

His full lips twisted in a smile quite devoid of amusement. 'I don't think, I know. There's only one person pulls that kind of stunt around here. The man who promised me the appointment to design and supervise the engineering works at the new Leisure Complex. Huh! That will be the bloody day! Pardon my French.'

'You don't think that he meant it? Whoever he was,' she added hastily.

'I'm not saying it aloud and I didn't tell that Detective Sergeant either. With friends like the man I'm thinking of, who needs enemas?'

It took Grace a few seconds to plumb the implications of the pun. She repressed a chuckle – he needed no encouragement – and instead filed the words away for repetition to Stuart. 'Who indeed?' she said.

'But I do know that when Charlie Gore was appointed QS for the school extension, that man went to Charlie and claimed that he had him to thank for the job while it was public knowledge that he'd argued against the appointment. He does that as a matter of routine. And now he's going round calling in what he claims to be favours so as to raise support and finance for the Leisure Complex. What I told the Sergeant and what I'm telling you is that I had no quarrel with Stuart Campbell. He's a good man. He asked a few awkward questions, but that was quite right and proper and I had answers for all of them.'

'Good for you!' Grace said. He was a much nicer person when he stopped laying on the conscious charm. 'Then you won't mind if I ask you whether you left the party before or after Stuart?'

He chuckled. 'You want my alibi?'

'Just information.'

'I don't mind at all but I'm not sure that I can tell you. Thinking back, and after seeing the photographs, I think that I probably left while he was having a pee in the Portaloo, because I think he moved away before I did but there was no sign of him when I reached the street. It took me about five minutes to walk to my car and I'd just reached it when I heard an ambulance. Whether it was the same ambulance, I wouldn't know, but I told the Sergeant just what I've told you and he'll probably check whether there was more than one ambulance in the area at the time.'

'And you didn't see anybody on the stairs or lurking in wait?'

'Once again, I'll tell you what I told the Sergeant. I didn't meet anybody on the stairs. I could hear the voices of men working and the chug of a cement mixer somewhere in the background. I wasn't paying any attention when I got outside, but I think there was a woman with a pram and a couple of workmen waiting for a delivery. Anybody else has faded away altogether.'

Grace nodded slowly. 'That's all I can think of for the moment. You'll let the police know if you think of anything else?' She drained her cup and prepared to get up. 'Thank you for the coffee.'

'One moment.' The charm made a sudden return. 'I wanted to ask you whether you'd care to come out for a meal one evening? Or perhaps go in to Inverness to the theatre?'

She might possibly have accepted the invitation, if only for the pleasure of showing Elaine that she did not have exclusive use of female pheromones, had her relationship with Stuart not been developing so satisfactorily. After all, a meal and an evening out were not offered her every day of the week. 'My evenings are pretty full,' she said.

'But do try. I'll give you a phone. I remember you so clearly from school. I was getting very interested in girls and I thought that you were quite the prettiest in your year.'

'I take that with a whole barrowload of salt,' she said, 'but thank you for saying it anyway. I seem to remember that you were much more taken up with chasing after

June somebody. And not without success, from what I heard.'

On her return home, she found Stuart in a more placid and even more affectionate mood. A fireside chair had been brought into his room and he had graduated to sitting up in it for much of the day. 'You are indeed a gem,' he said. 'I thought that you might be my perfect woman almost as soon as I set eyes on you, and now I know it for sure.' He cocked an eye at her. 'Or, in your view of the proprieties, is it too early for me to say that?'

'Say what you like,' Grace said. 'I'm not promising to answer in the same terms – you'll have to try it and wait to find out – but I'll enjoy listening to your stumbling attempts to seduce me with a golden tongue. It still won't gain you more than a kiss on the cheek.'

'That wasn't exactly on the cheek. Oh, well. Roll on the day when I can curl up into a taxi.'

Grace was beginning to envy him his easy release. The thought of his arousal was finding an echo in herself such as her old friend and sometime lover George Tullos, with all his absent-minded caresses, had never managed to evoke. 'It does seem a long time to wait for a free meal,' she said. 'Perhaps I could push you down to the town. I can think of one or two restaurants reasonably accessible to a wheelchair. I'm not quite so sure about pushing you back up the hill, however.'

He bubbled immediately with enthusiasm. 'Just get me down there. You wouldn't even have to push, just get me to the top of the hill and let me roll. We'll worry about getting me back later. We could hire one of the caddies from the golf club.' He looked at the wristwatch that he wore as a matter of habit, even in bed and with an illuminated bedside clock staring him in the face. A schoolmaster can become preoccupied with time. 'Damn!' he exclaimed. 'We've left it rather too late for this evening. How about tomorrow?'

'I'll look in my diary but I think I'm free.'

Mr and Mrs Gillespie seemed to be enjoying the sunshine in their garden, so Grace offered to prepare the evening meal. She had never enjoyed peeling potatoes and she was not displeased when a phone call interrupted her. She took it in the hall. A man's voice asked to speak to Stuart.

It took Grace some little while to find the cordless extension, which had been left on top of the television in the sitting room and hidden by a copy of the *Radio Times*. She tracked it down by using the pager facility and carried it through to Stuart. She had no intention of listening in, but as she was about to replace the main instrument in the hall she heard the voice say, 'This is Doug Burrard.' The name of one of her premier suspects, the man who had fought with Stuart over the sensuous Elaine, was enough to arrest her hand. The voice had a faint lisp but was otherwise indistinguishable from that of any other local man.

Grace put the receiver to her ear.

'What do you want?' said Stuart's voice. It did not sound friendly but nor was it particularly hostile.

'Just wanting to know how you're getting on.'

'I'm on the mend. Why would you care? The last time we met, we came to blows.'

'That's a rather extreme view of our disagreement. I wouldn't say blows exactly. Be fair. I don't remember anything that could fairly be called a blow. My recollection is that what happened between us was no more than a matter of male pride. To be honest, I seem to

189

remember that it was my fault that an exchange of insults turned into a pushing-match. You're going to make a full recovery from your fall?'

'My physiotherapist expects me to play tennis again.'

Grace felt a pang of guilt. She certainly expected Stuart to recover his mobility, but tennis might be rather much to ask, no matter what she had led Stuart to believe.

'That's excellent,' said Burrard's voice. 'I'll level with you. Your physio gave Elaine the impression that you might remain slightly crippled. That's why Elaine put her claws back into me. And I'll tell you frankly, I can well do without them. Having been dumped once, I've no desire to get involved again. She's running me ragged. May I tell her that you're going to recover your old vigour?'

Grace restrained herself from shouting down the phone.

'Tell her what you like,' Stuart said. He sounded amused. 'I was dumped too and I have no intention of taking her back. She's a thoroughly desirable girl –'

'She has everything in the right place,' Burrard put in. 'Warm and soft.'

'All silk-wrapped and smelling of violets,' Stuart agreed. 'And when she sets out to be seductive she could turn any man's head.'

Burrard was prepared to go further. 'She could suck you dry and blow you out in little bubbles,' he said. 'Men have sacrificed kingdoms for less. But when she isn't in that sort of mood, she's a bitch.'

'A virago.'

'A termagant.'

'Exactly. I wouldn't have her back,' Stuart said, 'if she was presented to me on black velvet, tied up with pink ribbons. And you can tell her I said so. Why don't you just tell her to go and bowl her hoop?'

'I've tried. God knows I've tried. But if I try it in public she starts to make a scene. And when we're alone together she only has to grab my hand and put it on her knee and I think, "Well, I suppose just once more won't do any harm." You know what I mean?'

'I know exactly what you mean.' Stuart's voice was not as lacking in enthusiasm as Grace would have wished. She made a face. 'I wouldn't worry too much. I'm still in touch with my friends and I hear that she's been seen with Duncan Macrae.'

'That one!' Burrard's voice said contemptuously. 'He's got so many strings to his bow, you'd think it was a harp. If it lasts a week, I'll bare my bum outside the cathedral the very next Sunday.'

Even that side issue did not divert Stuart from the male conspiracy. 'What was the name of that rather shady character in Dingwall or somewhere, the chap with the market garden, the slicked-down hair and all the money in the world? He seemed to fancy her. Pass her on to him.'

'I could try it, I suppose. I hope you're getting about better soon. Is that physio of yours any good?'

Grace held her breath.

'She is brilliant. And she's a living doll.'

Grace breathed again.

'You lucky devil! I can see why you don't want to take Elaine back off my hands. I suppose you'll tell me she was worth falling off a roof for?'

'Yes,' Stuart said reflectively, 'I think she was.'

'Sooner you than me. I call that doing it the hard way. Frankly, it seems like a rotten method of engineering an introduction. Why don't we meet for a pint, when you can get about?'

'We could do that,' Stuart said.

The conversation finished. Grace hung up the phone very quietly. She told herself that she was shocked to hear two men discussing women in such a cavalier manner. All the same, she was smiling. She punched the air. 'Yes!' she shouted silently.

19

Grace knew better than to dwell too much on a blossoming romance. She had been there before and had learned that to pin her hopes on the steadfastness of another would be to invite heartbreak. Woman might, according to Figaro, be a fickle jade but in Grace's experience Man was even more inclined towards a swift shift of affection. Stuart, she thought, would be rather more constant, but who knew what sirens might lurk in wait around the corner? Whatever would be would be. In the interval before sleep, she tried to keep her mind elsewhere, but the only other topic to offer itself was the mystery surrounding Stuart's fall which, combining as it did the baffling with the loss that might have been, was less than soporific. She drifted off to sleep with the memory of Stuart's voice in her mind and awoke with some fresh but half-digested thoughts about the mystery and an absolute conviction that Stuart would have changed his mind about her.

Stuart, however, did remain faithful. He was quieter than usual during his breakfast, treatment and bed-bath. Grace wondered whether his resentment had surfaced again, but when she prepared to leave him he caught her hand and retained it until he had planted a sensual kiss on each individual finger. Grace told herself that she was not going into a flutter like some Victorian maiden. She was made of sterner stuff.

She carried the cordless phone out of her patient's room. She could have used the main instrument in the kitchen but she wanted to follow up some of the ideas that the night had brought and this was one occasion when she wanted to be sure that she was not overheard. She secluded herself in the dining room and when her breathing had steadied she keyed the number of the *Daily Enquirer*. She asked for Ken Rosewell by name and, after some argument with a female voice prepared to defend its master from irate readers or correspondents, she was put through.

A voice came on the line that she thought of as brusque and forceful. Grace had nursed an injured Rugby player in Manchester and she detected a trace of the same accent. 'Mr Rosewell,' she said, 'I'm Grace Gillespie, Stuart Campbell's physiotherapist.'

There was a pause which she thought was due to caution rather than an inability to place the name. 'Is that so?' he said at last. 'How is he doing?'

'He's making good progress but his hands are still a long way short of using a keyboard.' She paused and fumbled for a form of words that would stay within the parameters of what she knew or could be reasonably sure of. 'Have you found anyone else to do the work for you?'

'Not yet.'

'So it isn't urgent?'

'I think perhaps it's about to become very urgent. I anticipate difficulty finding anyone else as skilled and yet as trustworthy and discreet as Mr Campbell.'

She decided that they had been fencing for long enough. 'I could probably use the keyboard for him if he told me what to do.'

'You'd better let me speak to him.'

'I can't.' Grace said. 'Mr Rosewell, Stuart isn't speaking to anybody. He was threatened, but that isn't the whole of it. He could get help and protection from the police, but my reading of him is that he's afraid to be open with them. And the only possible reason that I can think of would be because of the legality of whatever he was doing for you. Would that be possible?'

There was a pause. 'You can't expect me to comment on that.'

'I suppose not, but I can draw my own conclusions.' As she spoke, it occurred to Grace that she might be following Stuart into a previously unsuspected lion's den. 'In case I'm inviting trouble for myself, I've left a statement of all I know and suspect with a solicitor.'

'That seems sensible.' His voice was expressionless. 'And where do you stand in all this?'

'I'm going to marry him,' she said, to her own surprise. 'So I look to you for help.'

'If he's asked you to marry him...'

Grace decided to be honest. After all, Stuart and Mr Rosewell might well be speaking on the phone soon. 'He hasn't,' she said. 'I haven't told him yet, but I'm going to marry him whether he asks me or not. I know that he'll jump at it. This may sound a bit like an ancient joke, but I am quite resolved.'

Amusement crept into the other's voice. 'Miss Gillespie, all that you say may be true, but you are still only a voice on the phone to me and I'm not prepared to open up to any old voice on the phone, however attractive its accent. I suggest that you stall things along for a few hours. I'll do what I can from this end. If I can get the pressure taken off, will you do as you suggested and work the keyboard for Mr Campbell?'

'Yes. If I'm satisfied that the activities are neither illegal nor immoral.'

'Miss Gillespie, I look forward to working with you.'

With that she decided to be content, for a few hours and no longer.

The phone rang again as soon as she had disconnected and she concluded that somebody had been using the call-waiting facility. The voice that spoke turned out to have the deep resonance of Detective Inspector Welles. 'I'll be in Dornoch this afternoon,' he said. 'It's important that I see you. Will you be in?'

'What's it about?'

'I may as well tell you,' he said slowly, 'if only to give you time to work on Mr Campbell. DS Ballintore is getting nowhere with the various assaults. My boss – Superintendent Largs – is quite sure that Mr Campbell is holding onto all the information we need; and he's not the man to wait for a witness to make up his mind to be helpful while the culprits cover their tracks. If we don't get a result soon, Mr Largs is going to lose patience and come through to interview Mr Campbell himself. He wants this case cleared up. He'll put your patient through the wringer and, believe me, he's an expert. And if he doesn't get the co-operation he expects, he's quite capable of charging Mr Campbell with obstructing the police, failing to report a crime and several other offences.'

Grace found herself trying to speak around a sudden lump in her throat. 'If Mr Campbell is being threatened, that might be all that's needed to make somebody turn the threats into more of the same kind of acts.'

'If there were no other way to bring out the evidence, Mr Largs would feel quite justified in taking that risk – after taking precautions of course. But it wouldn't come to that. The threat is almost always enough to get the most reluctant of honest witnesses talking. After that, we can take effective action.'

Grace felt hollowness where previously there had been a warm and comfortable feeling. Superintendent

Largs sounded like an ogre and not even the fact that she knew and liked his wife made him any less formidable. The prospect of Stuart, in his present nervous state, being turned inside out by such a man was unnerving enough, but the thought that Stuart might still be blaming her for feeding him to the ogre was not to be borne. She had a vague idea that a firm repetition of 'No comment' might fend off a hostile interrogation, but surely the Law must have some mechanism for dealing with a sullen witness?

'Can you win me a day or two?' she asked.

'I doubt it. He wants my report on his desk tomorrow morning.'

She tried to sound angry rather than defensive. 'You want me to work on Stuart but you don't give me any time to do it. Will you still be in Dornoch this evening?'

'As it happens, yes. I have to wait over to see the Procurator Fiscal about another matter and he won't be back from court in Thain until about six.'

'Mr Campbell and I will be having dinner in the town this evening. Would you join us for coffee? Or for dinner, if you think it would be appropriate?'

'Coffee would be fine, thank you. About eight?'

'Perfect!' And she meant it. At least there would now be a man to help her up the hill with the wheelchair. She gave him directions and as soon as the call finished she phoned the restaurant to book a table with space for a wheelchair and a patient with a protruding leg.

She called Ken Rosewell again. This time the secretary put her through at once. 'It's become very urgent,' she said. 'Detective Inspector Welles wants to see him this evening and I've no control over what Stuart will or won't say.'

'Don't worry. I've made a call and I'll make another. If

they don't produce immediate results, tell Mr Campbell to say nothing else and to refer Detective Inspector – Welles, did you say? – to Mr Huntington Pride at the Home Office. But don't mention that name to anybody, even to Stuart, unless you absolutely have to.'

She said nothing to Stuart about these developments and he never asked her about the telephone traffic. She busied herself about the house for the next few hours, did some laundry and ironed her one good cocktail dress. She brought forward his evening treatment to mid-afternoon and then began preparations for their outing. With a little help from the patient, she got him shaved and tidily dressed. She had developed some talent with the scissors during her years of caring for the immobile and she even managed a little overdue trimming of his hair and beard. She left him sitting in the fireside chair with his leg up on a stool while she took her shower and dressed, quickly but tidily. Her hair took a little longer. For once she applied more than the basic minimum of makeup and a touch of perfume.

When they were ready to leave, Mrs Gillespie answered a sudden ring at the phone. She brought the cordless handset to Stuart. 'It's the hospital.'

Stuart took the phone. 'Yes, speaking...' There was a long pause while he listened. Grace had had the impression that he had put aside his worries in anticipation of an evening of relaxation and amorous whispering, but she saw the haggard expression make a return. 'It may be some time before I can visit, I'm in a wheelchair... It's that bad? Please keep me posted.' He disconnected and looked up at Grace. 'My uncle's had a stroke, a bad one. You heard me say that I can't visit yet, but the ward sister said that he wouldn't recognise anybody at the moment. He's paralysed down one side and his speech has gone. They think he'll recover some of his faculties but he'll need a lot of time and nursing.'

Grace broke a desolate silence. 'Stuart, I'm so sorry. But there's nothing you can do for him at the moment. And our table is booked.'

Mrs Gillespie had lingered. 'You certainly wouldn't be doing him any good by staying here and moping,' she said briskly. 'Maybe the news will be better in the morning. Put it out of your minds until then. Run along and enjoy your dinner.' She paused in the doorway. 'That's what your uncle would want.'

'Your mother's partly right,' Stuart told Grace. 'I'm not sure what Uncle Duncan would want.' He gave a short and bitter laugh. 'In his Calvinistic way, he'd probably disapprove of a couple spending good money and dining out in public when they could eat at home for a tenth of the price, but we'll go anyway. What he doesn't know can't hurt him. I don't know what else I can say. "Wagons roll" perhaps?'

'The dog-sled people cry "Mush" I think,' said Grace.

His smile made a tremulous return. 'Mush, then.'

The day had clouded over but rain, which would have ruined her plans, stayed away. Stuart was transferred to the wheelchair and, with a little help from Mr Gillespie, the front door step was negotiated. Grace's parents had taken to their guest and her father was prepared to help push the wheelchair into the town, but it was pointed out that the rest of the route was flat or downhill. They accomplished the journey in silence. Stuart seemed, as usual, to be wrapped in his worries and Grace was trying to anticipate every twist and turn of events that might be to come.

In the restaurant, a corner table had been reserved. If

he sat at a slight angle, Stuart's leg could project without tripping up the waitress or any other customers. The place was quietly bustling and there was background music, so they could talk without being overheard. They managed to chat about generalities between ordering drinks and choosing their meal and a bottle of wine. Stuart, who was still sensitive about his disabilities, limited himself to food that could be cut with a fork, to avoid the humiliation of having Grace cut his food up for him as if he were a child or an incompetent. The waitress had known Grace and had been a pupil of Stuart's. She relayed their orders and then returned to gossip about the past. Grace thought that the lady was also ready to burst with curiosity about her relationship with Stuart. Doubtless the word about Stuart's accident and Grace's enquiries had stimulated local interest. Grace was wearing an assortment of bracelets to hide the welts that still disfigured her wrists, but the bruise on Stuart's forehead was still attracting attention.

When the meal had arrived and they were private at last and secure from interruptions, Stuart began to eat in silence. Suddenly he said, 'This changes everything.'

Grace had seen this coming and her arguments were ready. 'Your uncle's stroke? I'm not prepared to accept that it changes anything. Except for Mr Cameron, of course.'

'I think you will.' He put down his fork and looked at her seriously. 'This is the moment when I should hold my tongue. I should walk off nobly into the sunset, leaving you unaware of the enormous sacrifice I've just made.' Grace started to speak but he hurried on. 'All right. I can't walk off into the sunset, or anywhere else, until you've done a lot more work on me. So I should trundle myself off into the sunset. But I can't do that. I'm not a storybook hero. I'm being stupid and inconsiderate and I'm breaking all the rules, but this has to be said aloud just once or I'll burst. After that, we must both try to forget it. Perhaps it's a blessing that this happened now and not, say, tomorrow, because I was going to tell you tonight that you're my dream woman.'

Grace was torn between concern and amusement. 'And now you're not going to?'

'How can I? I was going to tell you that you're not just sexually magnetic; you have an inner serenity and you understand. Without being less than yourself, you adapt. We have a common wavelength. You're stately, that's the only word to describe you, and yet that hides a sense of humour that delights me. With you I could let my hair down, rant at the world, be humorous, be vulgar, be happy or sad, be anything I want to be; and you'd take it all in your stride. You were the one woman I could imagine spending the rest of my life with. That's what I was going to say.'

'I don't think that I've changed much during the last hour or two,' Grace said.

'Of course not. And my feelings haven't changed at all. It may be all wrong of me, but I couldn't bear to have you misunderstand.' He reached for her hand and took it in his weak grasp. She was too slow to pull it out of reach. 'I... I was going to hand you my heart with a ribbon round it and ask you to keep it for me. I was going to ask you to stay with me always, for God's sake. I was going to ask you to marry me. But you must surely see that this changes everything. My uncle's going to be bedridden, a vegetable, for the rest of his life.'

'And that changes what? So he'll need nursing. In case you hadn't noticed, that's what I do. And stroke patients make amazing recoveries these days.'

'Not always.'

'Stuart,' she said, 'suppose that this hadn't happened yet. Suppose that your uncle had had his stroke while we were on our honeymoon. What then? Would you have divorced me?'

He released her hand and resumed his meal. 'But you have your career.'

'Always moving on, adapting to new people and their ways. Making friends, human or animal, and leaving them behind. Being looked down on or up to but never quite being seen as the real me.' She locked eyes with him. 'You listen to me, Stuart Campbell. Do you not think that I might have longed to settle down, in the land of my birth, put down roots again and stay with the same faces? Perhaps work in a garden and know that I'll still be there to see it flower next spring? Have a dog of my own instead of walking somebody else's? Have somebody to love? Perhaps even a family? With you in particular? Don't you think that nursing your uncle would be an infinitesimal price to pay for all of that?'

Hope flickered in his face again and then died. 'I was right first time,' he said. 'I should have stayed quiet. And yet, I'll always be both sad and yet comforted by what you've just said. But it can't be. Even if I dared ask you to nurse my uncle indefinitely –'

The waitress returned to remove their plates and deliver the sweet course. Grace, who had seen her own arguments tidily laid out before her, could cheerfully have strangled the woman. When they were alone again, she said, 'If the stroke's as serious as that, he won't get home for a long time. I'll have you on your feet and back at work before then. The situation then will be what? I'll have one patient. Well, that's the story of my life. I'll also have a husband,' Grace said firmly, 'who is out for most of every weekday but can give a little help when he's at home. I'll be cooking for three, which is no big deal. Your house has all the helpful household machines and gadgets I could think of and, if you ever think I'm overworked, Geordie's sister from next door but one can come in and clean. So don't give me any of that...' She paused, hesitating between words. She wanted to put her message forcefully but the only suitable word was a very rude one and was it perhaps too early in their relationship? Stuart had not balked at a rude word, but only when an essential element in a genuinely funny joke.

'It isn't crap.' Stuart said, showing for the first time a sign of the telepathy that can develop between two people who are on identical wavelengths.

She was spared the need for immediate comment. Emotions were fighting for expression on Stuart's face but they were interrupted. Detective Inspector Welles was slipping between the tables. He fetched another chair and dumped himself down opposite Stuart. Without preamble he turned to Grace. 'How in God's name did you know?' he asked her.

20

Grace felt an immediate lifting of the heart. It was followed by an upsurge of impatience. How like a policeman, to come crashing in at the crucial moment! But first things first. Her guesses had been good – or were she and the Detective Inspector at cross-purposes? With a quick mental effort she sorted her priorities. Just let her get the threat to Stuart out of the way and she could deal with his silly scruples about the more important matter.

'I was right then?' she asked.

Detective Inspector Welles blinked at her. 'Perhaps I was being premature. I'm only making a reasoned guess at what you were thinking, so I can hardly be sure whether you were right or miles off the mark. But somebody has been busy on the phone and you're my only suspect. It's quite clear that you knew or thought you knew something and, on the basis of what's been happening today, my guess is that you were smack on target.' He looked from one to the other. His usual friendly air had been replaced by a look of uncertainty. 'I'm walking on eggshells here. My orders are that the topic is to be treated as totally confidential, even from my colleagues. If any of my seniors tries to force the issue, I'm to refer them to a very senior official; that's how serious it is.'

He paused and looked meaningfully at Grace, who said 'Wow!' It seemed to be expected of her.

'Obviously,' the DI resumed, 'I can't keep from you what you already know and, if you already know most of it, it may be better that I tell you or confirm the rest so that your curiosity doesn't cause you to make any more waves.'

'And also as a bribe for our silence?' Grace suggested.

The smile made a momentary and tentative reappearance. 'That too. So tell me what you know and how you found it out and we'll see whether we can't fill in any gaps for each other.'

'Fair enough,' Grace said after a moment of thought. 'That seems reasonable. You come clean with me and neither Stuart nor I will ever say a word.' She remembered that she still required a push up the hill with the wheelchair. She looked around. The restaurant had fallen quiet, which suited her line of argument very well. 'But is this really the place? It seems a little bit public for such a discussion. I promised you coffee but we could take it at my home.'

'We make quite good coffee at the nick,' the Inspector suggested.

'Not as good as at home,' Grace said firmly. The police station was at the foot of the hill and once she had spilled what beans she had to spill she might not be able to count on a friendly push. She signalled for the bill.

Stuart had been looking from one to the other in puzzlement. 'Is somebody going to tell me what the hell's going on?' he asked.

Grace patted his hand. 'When we get home. Have patience a little longer. But everything's going to be all right, I promise you. Everything.'

Stuart was still far from satisfied. He seemed to have paled. 'You can't possibly make such a promise and be sure of keeping it. I don't think you know what you've done.'

'I know better than you do, my dear. And you must

know that I wouldn't do anything to harm you or make a promise I couldn't keep.'

It was a measure of the growing depth of Stuart's feeling for Grace that his protests subsided, but the haggard look was still there.

When the bill arrived, Grace produced her credit card but Stuart overruled her with unaccustomed firmness. She had intended the meal to be her treat but she realised in time that this was the ritual courtship of the male feeding the female. If Stuart was still following that path, it seemed that he must trust her not to have landed him in trouble with the Law. The glow of satisfaction reached her fingers and toes.

As they passed the police station, Grace said, 'We'll need the photographs. Where are they now?'

The Detective Inspector set the brake on the wheelchair. 'I'll fetch them.'

He emerged again within seconds and gave the box to the passenger to hold. With his help, the short hill was soon ascended. When he seemed quite willing to continue, Grace surrendered control of the wheelchair to him. Policemen, after all, were public servants. They walked in silence through the silent evening.

The house was almost as quiet. Only the whisper of electrical equipment broke the hush. Grace recalled that her parents had intended to visit friends and expected to return late. She led the way into the sitting room and switched on the electric fire. The artificial coals cheered the room immediately, in keeping with her rising mood. Stuart remained in the wheelchair, which was parked in a place of honour. She darted through to the kitchen to put coffee on. When she returned to the sitting room, she was pushing a light trolley which, in addition to the coffee, supported a bottle of brandy, glasses and a selection of mixers. The occasion seemed to demand it. The two men had been making disjointed talk about football, a subject that she knew bored Stuart to distraction.

'I don't know about anyone else,' she said, 'but I'm ready for another drink. It has been quite a day. You may as well have one of your cigarettes,' she told Stuart. 'Mum's visitors have been smoking in here.' She gave herself a brandy with lemonade. Stuart took his neat. The Inspector was persuaded to accept a small brandy and soda. The festive air boosted Grace's confidence.

When she had finished dispensing, the Inspector took a sip of his coffee and nodded approval. 'You were right,' he said. 'This is better coffee than at the nick. Now perhaps you could get around to answering the question I posed nearly half an hour ago.'

'I suppose so,' Grace said. 'Really, in the end it was complicated; but if you looked at the bits in the right sequence it made perfect sense. Going back to the beginning, I couldn't believe that Stuart's injuries were the result of a simple fall. I tried to imagine how he could have got the bruises to his back and head and also the serious knee and elbow damage without injuring his shoulders, hips and pelvis. The only picture that made sense was that somebody hit him from behind, then deliberately broke his knees and elbows with some sort of cosh or a padded hammer and threw him from the level immediately below the roof. I was in no doubt that he had also been very convincingly threatened.'

Inspector Welles gave Stuart a look of reproof. 'Is that the truth?' Stuart hesitated and then nodded. 'If you'd made a complaint to us at the time, we could have given you protection.'

'You don't understand,' Stuart said. 'They threatened that, if I even looked in the direction of the police, they'd give my girlfriend the same treatment. I never saw their faces, so there would have been no evidence to offer a court. The protection you could offer wouldn't have amounted to very much and the law doesn't allow me to protect myself. Frankly, it gives my assailants more rights than it gives me.'

'But even after Elaine broke with you –' Grace began.

'When they came back and attacked my uncle, they threatened to do the same to you. But there was more than that.'

Grace decided that the subject of his concern for her could wait for another time. 'Of course there was,' she said. 'You were determined that the police must not be brought into it. That worried me, but, you see, it was a matter of faith. I was quite sure that you had done nothing that a reasonable person would regard as criminal, not even something to be really ashamed of. You're just not that sort of person; you're too benevolent. You mean so well.'

'Thank you for that much,' Stuart said. 'But it was a rash assumption. If you'd been wrong you could have brought the wrath of God down on me. Perhaps you have, anyway.'

'You're welcome; and I'm sure that I haven't. My first thought was that you'd been involved in some worthy but illegal cause. I couldn't see you as a vigilante, exactly, but I could imagine you committing a little Robin Hoodery, if you thought that the cause was a just one. But that didn't seem to add up and, as I told you, I decided that it had to be woman trouble. Somebody's husband; or, more probably, a male relative of one of the parties, hoping to spare the husband the pain of finding out. You were keeping quiet to protect a lady's name. That was just the sort of quixotic idiocy I could believe of you. But you convinced me that it wasn't like that.'

'Romantic rubbish,' Stuart said, but it was said kindly, with fondness.

Grace returned her attention to the Inspector. 'I puzzled over it. Then I remembered that somebody – Joan McTaggart, I think it was – said that Stuart had demonstrated in class how easy it was to "hack" into somebody else's secrets. She was careful to explain that you didn't tell them *how* to do it,' she added to Stuart. 'Just that it was possible. Well, I'd noticed the number of the Ken Rosewell who phoned you. He seemed to expect your help and you choked him off rather abruptly. I heard his name on the amplifier and the number was staring at me from the little screen. The area code looked familiar and I associated it with another journalist. When I began to get ideas, I called the number and discovered that it belonged to the *Daily Enquirer*. I know that the paper's right at the forefront of investigative journalism. If a politician takes a big bribe or a financier pulls off a swindle, he first knows he's been rumbled when he sees his face on the front page. And then there follows a major trial and the paper sells an extra million copies. So I started wondering what sort of relationship you could have with the features editor.

'The paper had to get its information from somewhere. Hacking would be illegal, but it would provide a starting-point from which an investigative journalist could begin digging; and what he dug up by legal means would be useable. I could just imagine some former pupil, now an employee of the paper, mentioning Stuart's name to Mr Rosewell. Exposing misdeeds of the fat cats would appeal to Stuart but it would be outside the strict borderline of the law. If that was why he was attacked, I could understand his reluctance to speak to the police. Also, before Stuart was to be attacked, somebody had to know that Stuart was gathering evidence against him. That suggested a leak from the newspaper office – or somewhere else. It seemed to me that the kingpin was Mr Rosewell. So I phoned him. I didn't know or care whether he called in some favours or spread money around, but I was sure that he could help and I may have hinted that he'd better do just that or somebody would do some talking that might not be the kind he appreciates. I gather that he did take action?'

'That he certainly did,' said Inspector Welles. He hesitated, looking from one to the other, before going on. 'You've been frank and we wouldn't want you think that Rosewell had, in your words, been "spreading money around". He phoned a contact in the Home Office who phoned another in the Scottish Office and the result was that a very senior official indeed contacted me, personally, just over an hour ago. And this is where confidentiality takes over. I want your assurance that neither of you will ever discuss this with anybody else, anybody at all.'

'You already have it,' Stuart pointed out. Grace nodded.

Detective Inspector Welles seemed to be reassured. 'The fact is that the *Daily Enquirer* has been hand in glove with the uppermost echelons of the police all along. The police are constrained by a thousand rules limiting how they can obtain evidence if it's to be admissible in court. But if a journalist tells them, or they read in their daily paper, that So-and-so has a bank account in his grandmother's name and half a million has just been paid into it from a laundered source, they have a chance of getting a court order. The police can then obtain the same information quite legally for themselves. The paper will protect the identity of its sources, come what may. So a very blind eye has been turned in this direction and the powers that be would prefer to keep it that way. There have been some successful prosecutions and some surprising resignations for improbable health or family reasons. The less reputable members of the establishment are hastily cleaning up their various acts. Most of the top brass would very much like this to continue but definitely do not want the methods revealed. Others of them are among those who are busy act-cleaning. A prime case of the end justifying the means.'

The importance of what was being said was becoming clear to Stuart only slowly. 'I'm in the clear, then?' he said.

That would have been overstating the case. 'Provided you don't open your mouth, nor will anybody else,' said the Inspector. 'If the facts come out, a prosecution may become inevitable. So you would be well advised to keep a close guard on your tongue.' He began to show signs of restiveness.

'Do you know which particular bigwig was responsible this time?' Grace asked.

Inspector Welles, who had hoped not to be asked the question, sagged back into his chair. 'Do you?' he retorted.

'Stuart must know who he was working on up to the time when he was attacked. But I think you owe it to me to confirm what I think. I suspect Councillor Allnith. He's raising money for the Leisure Complex, which my father says is unlikely to be profitable. Mr Rosewell said that Stuart's contribution was about to become urgent.

212

The closing date for investors is at the beginning of next week. My guess is that the Councillor has been siphoning off the money as fast as it comes in and that he plans to be a long way abroad before that fact comes out. He was at the ceremony when Stuart had his fall. Could we have another look at the photographs?'

'Yes, of course.' The Inspector produced the box, now showing signs of wear.

The room was lit softly by wall lamps. Grace got up to switch on the central light. The cosy room suddenly looked stark. She took only seconds to find the shots she wanted. 'Here we are. I was misled at first by seeing that the Councillor was still among the guests on the roof after Stuart had left. In this shot, I thought that he was scratching his ear.' Grace looked at Stuart, to find that he was gaping at her. 'Stuart, when you asked about that photograph of me holding a telephone, I nearly saw the whole thing. Then I had a dream about talking into a photograph.' She sighed. 'The penny's only just dropped. If you look very closely, I think you can see that he's speaking into one of those new, very small mobile phones.'

Inspector Welles almost snatched a small group of glossy prints out of her hand. 'You're absolutely right,' he said. 'You can't see the phone but, once you have the thought in your mind, the attitude says it all. I've studied these photographs until my eyes popped and I never noticed that. So we can suppose that he was speaking to some confederate and saying, "Get ready, he's on the way down."'

'So I'm right?'

The Inspector hesitated and then shrugged. 'It will be all over the media tomorrow anyway. We have a warrant and we intend to pick him up in the morning.

Mr Rosewell gave us the name and the facts as far as they'd come out. The more detailed information –?'

'Is at my bank,' Stuart said. 'I didn't want disks or printouts with that sort of material on them at home.'

'Very wise. You had better have Miss Gillespie collect them from your bank and send them to Mr Rosewell first thing tomorrow morning, so that the information can reach us from a source which the newspaper will refuse to disclose, all as per usual. So now we have the whole story, with the sole exception of just who the Councillor was phoning. I don't suppose that he'll ever give us their names.'

Grace had recovered the photographs. The shots of the solitary figure lying broken on the roof were easily isolated. 'When you look at this one,' she said, 'the eye is drawn to the figure lying twisted in the middle of the roof. In fact, the edge of the roof is included and you get an oblique view down into part of the street. You tend not to notice it because it's only a triangle and it's in shadow – in fact, the eye can pass over it, thinking that it's the raised arm of the foreground figure. But if you look into it you can make out people there, though they're very tiny, and three of them are looking up, because the fuss and excitement had begun. Another two are walking away towards what looks like the back corner of a Land Rover. That seems to me to be unlikely behaviour. If there's some excitement going on and other people are looking upwards you'd have to be remarkably incurious to walk off before you knew what it was about.'

'Let me see that, please.' The Inspector almost snatched the glossy print. From his wallet, he produced a very thin, plastic magnifier and he studied the images intently. 'I don't believe it,' he said at last, 'and yet I'm almost sure. Excuse me. I want to make a phone call and I want to be free to speak my mind.'

He fumbled in his pocket as he left the room. His expression was grim.

21

There was silence between them at first, a silence that neither knew how to break. Grace got up and killed the central lights. The gentler glow from the wall brackets seemed to make communication easier. Stuart sighed and was the first to speak. 'So I've been worrying myself sick for weeks and putting us at risk, all for nothing.' He gave a tiny snort of bitter amusement. 'I'm an idiot – what am I?'

'You are not an idiot,' Grace said hotly. 'You weren't to know that the police were hand in glove with the *Daily Enquirer*.'

'Perhaps I should have guessed it when there were no repercussions after our earlier scoops.' He stretched. Watching him relax by degrees, she realised she had never seen him without the inner tension that she had put down to his nature and his injuries. 'Well, well. Anybody can be wrong once but I seem to have managed it rather more often than that. Your one wrong was about my injuries. There was no hammer. They... they jumped on my elbows and then rolled me over onto my back and jumped on my knees.'

She closed her eyes as though that would block out the picture. All the same, it was good that he could now speak about it. 'And you took it in silence?'

'I was still winded and half stunned.'

Grace could sympathise. She had been in the same condition. Perhaps that was part of the *modus operandi*. 'From the blow on the head?'

'Yes.' He dropped his voice. Grace guessed that he was ashamed of his next confession. 'And, to be honest, I was scared witless.'

'Anyone would be.' She switched to what she hoped would be a happier topic. 'I trust that you weren't working for Mr Rosewell out of the goodness of your heart? You deserve to get something out of it.'

Stuart cheered up at once. He smiled comfortably. 'Ken Rosewell always paid up and paid handsomely.' He produced the packet and took out a cigarette.

'I always thought you seemed very affluent for a teacher. There are signs of money in all that electric gadgetry and you didn't get your house or car for trading stamps.'

Grace paused. She had given some thought to her attitude towards his smoking. She wanted him to live happily ever after or, if that were not possible, at least for a very long time. Her past had been filled with animals – it was in the nature of things that anyone needing the services of a resident physiotherapist was unlikely to be fit to walk the dog. She had even been cajoled into keeping up the advanced dog training for an incapacitated patient who had broken a hip by falling over his young spaniel. One of the foremost rules – never to give an order unless you could enforce it – seemed just as applicable to people. Stuart would be out of her sight for most of the working day. 'Now that you can get out in the wheelchair,' she said, 'I think you should go back to not smoking indoors. It would be better for you, it would help you to limit your smoking and the smell wouldn't bother anybody else. And it would please me,' she added, 'which should count for something. How would you like a kiss?'

He blinked at the apparent change of subject but looked pleased and expectant. 'Very much.'

'A beard smelling of smoke does not attract. Limit yourself to outdoors or lose the beard.'

He considered the proposition gravely and then smiled. 'I think I can go along with that.'

'Which?'

'I'll think about it.' He thought. 'Both.'

'Think of it,' she said, 'as a small price to pay for –' she hesitated and then plunged onward '– for the best sex you'll ever have.'

A variety of expressions chased each other across his face, too quickly for her to identify with any certainty. Surprise predominated, followed immediately by delight, which as quickly faded. 'It seems that I'll have to wait some time for my reward.'

She hesitated. Was she being too forward and giving the false impression that she had a lurid past? And could she live up to her boast? She decided to strike anyway while the iron was hot. She pulled the wheelchair closer and took his hand. 'Not necessarily. We're adults,' she said. 'If we were ten years younger we would probably have grappled each other into bed straight away and got around to talking about it afterwards if at all. But we can discuss it in a sensible manner. There are ways and ways. I had a hip replacement patient once. Don't look so scandalised,' she said, laughing. 'I didn't sleep with him. He and his wife were keen to get back to normal relations so I asked a consultant therapist for advice on their behalf.'

'Did it work?'

'They seemed delighted. And what I told them – and which they later repeated back to me as though it was their own discovery – included the fact that you don't have to break the bed. In fact, violent may get you there quicker but slow and gentle lasts longer and is better when it arrives.'

He returned the still unlit cigarette to the packet. She could guess why he was moving uncomfortably in the wheelchair. 'I'm sure you're right,' he said. 'I'm getting excited, just thinking about it. It must be the healthy diet you've had me on. That and the L-word.'

'Don't think about it, then,' she said. 'Think about the L-word. Can't you say it aloud?'

He swivelled the chair round and grasped both her hands. She noticed that his clasp was gaining strength. He released one in order to stroke her cheek. 'I can say it aloud. Love, love, love. I've used it before but I never meant it like this. Let's dream a little. Let's go back to my house as soon as we can. *Come live with me and be my love.*' His voice began to fade. 'At least until –'

'Until what? Until your uncle comes home?'

'Yes.'

'I've told you before, I'm not afraid to take you on, and your uncle with you.' She leaned forward and kissed him. 'I want to stay with you, look after you, married or not, and if your uncle comes with the deal so be it. Why are you so afraid of a longer commitment?'

'I'm not afraid of the commitment. Or perhaps I am. But I'm not afraid to promise you anything you want, you must surely know that. What I am afraid of is entering a commitment that circumstances won't let us stick with.'

She withdrew her hands and pointed a finger at him. 'What you're afraid of is that I'd find the pair of you too much of a burden. Or is it that you're afraid I'll think you're just looking for a free nurse? You can go on paying my salary, if you like, but I warn you, I'm expensive. More expensive than a wife.'

He smiled at last and made another grab for her hands. She let him capture them. 'I want to have you around for years and years and years,' he said. 'But I don't want to make you make any promises. I want you to be free to leave, if ever you can't bear it any longer.'

'I'll make the promises anyway,' she told him, 'and I'll feel just as bound by them as if I'd given them in marriage. But forget it for tonight.'

'Ah yes,' he said. 'Tonight.'

Rather to her relief, because some things are better not spoken aloud, the Inspector chose that moment to return to the room. He resumed his seat and looked at Grace curiously. 'You've been strangely, almost suspiciously, omniscient about everything else. Who do you think was walking away from the building?'

'Some hireling of Councillor Allnith,' Grace said. 'Probably somebody who already had a grudge against Stuart.'

'But who?'

'You tell me.'

He smiled, teasing her. 'My lips are sealed, remember?'

Grace's mood was by now too good to let the teasing irritate her. She recalled one face that had vanished from the throng in the photographs before Stuart's departure, the boy who had been suspended from school. 'I don't have nearly enough information so I'll be guessing. But my guess would be... Dean Murray.' She produced the name with a flourish.

As soon as she spoke she could tell by Inspector Welles's face that she was wrong, but before he could trump her ace Stuart spoke. 'Don't let him lead you around in circles,' he said. 'Dean Murray has a perfect alibi for the occasion when the policeman and you and my uncle and I were all attacked and my house was invaded. Anyway, his build would have been quite wrong for either assault.

'Your mother told me about his alibi and she got it from a friend in the fiscal's office, so it's probably true and not just a wild rumour. He was in the police station all day when we were attacked. It seems that he was driving his father's Land Rover quite illegally the day before on the single-track road past Embo and he came up behind a farmworker on a tractor, towing a trailer laden with straw bales – the big, round ones. The driver could have pulled into a passing place to let him go by but he didn't have that much consideration and when Dean used his horn he got a two-fingered salute in return. The trailer was overloaded and the tractor was crawling, so Dean stopped the Land Rover, got out and ran after it, opening his penknife as he ran.' Stuart snorted with laughter. 'He used his penknife to cut the binder twine on the straw bales. Then he backed the Land Rover, turned in a field gate and went round by the main road, leaving the farmer to pick up a mountain of loose straw. The police chivvied the farmer about obstructing the highway and he'd recognised young Murray, so he made a complaint.'

Grace was laughing with him. 'I think better of young Dean,' she said. 'We've all wanted to do something like that, or worse, to a tractor-driver. Few of us dare.' She raised an eyebrow at the Inspector. 'So who were our attackers?'

'I can tell you that,' Stuart said quickly. 'The Morrison brothers. Despite the ski masks, I recognised their builds and voices. I just didn't dare to do anything about it at the time. I could have identified them and pressed a prosecution, but I'd have been left wondering when they were going to come back for another and worse go at me or any current friends of mine. They are a vicious pair. More than vicious, evil.'

Grace shivered, remembering her ordeal. 'I go along with that description,' she said.

'You can leave that aspect of it to us,' the Inspector said.

'You reckon? The police do not have a very good record of protecting the innocent, nor of allowing them to protect themselves.'

For the first time since Grace first met him, Inspector Welles lost his disarming air of benevolence and she saw how he might look to a recalcitrant offender. 'Yes, I do reckon,' he said coldly. 'The sheriff sent them to the High Court for sentencing, because they'd made threats against you from the dock. That should have been warning enough. But they came after you again, twice. Perhaps for money, but spite certainly played a part. Now, I'm not asking you, I'm telling you. You will identify them and testify against them again. The facts will count very heavily against them. As repeat offenders, the courts will deal severely with them on top of their present sentences and this time they will not be given day release without strict supervision, if at all. I would also expect the court to give them a serious word of warning. If that doesn't seem to be enough, Mr Largs will give them a warning of his own and, believe me, when he warns you you're warned. Anyway, with nobody around to pay them for their efforts, even the Morrisons aren't mad enough to invite being sentenced yet again as doubly repeat offenders.'

'I hope you're right,' Stuart said.

Grace decided that, when the time came, she would keep a large dog and there would be a heavy stick behind each outer door, just in case. 'Well, I think you're a cheat,' she said. 'You assured me, through your wife, that the Morrisons were still firmly inside.'

The Inspector looked properly abashed. 'I believed it at the time. When I enquired, I was told that their parole had been turned down. Nobody bothered to mention that they were being let out on day release and were supposed to be working on a farm. The signs are that they had the farmer totally intimidated, so they could borrow his Land Rover and buzz off for the whole day without a word being said. They will not be out on day release tomorrow,' he added grimly, 'nor for a long time to come.'

'And the Councillor?' Grace asked.

'We'll gather him up in the morning.'

'You're forgetting one thing,' she said. 'He has a source of information in the newspaper office or – forgive me for suggesting it – in the police. Otherwise, how did he know that Stuart was looking into his finances in the first place? He probably knows by now that the beans have been spilled. He could be anywhere by morning.'

'Oh Jesus!' said the Inspector. He sprang to his feet. 'You could be right again. I hope you're not, but you could be. I must go. If it's not too late at night by the time I've prevented him doing a runner, I'll look back with several more questions. If we can't put our hands on him straight away, I'll come back and post a guard. Don't move, I'll let myself out.'

'Time we put you back to bed,' Grace said.

'Alone as usual, I suppose?'

'We'll see.' She took pity on him. Also, she could feel desire for him, deep inside herself but ready to rouse. She was doubly euphoric, from the wine and with the end to the danger. 'I don't expect my parents back yet.

Not that they'd be particularly shocked. I think they've been picturing me leading a life of depravity while I've been away, which I assure you is a very long way from the truth.'

'I never doubted it.'

'Of course you didn't. But I don't suppose they expect us to stop at holding hands.'

She trundled the wheelchair through into his room and set about preparing him for the night. When he was stripped, she washed him lovingly. His lack of response did not worry her. She could tell that he was thinking with determination about anything asexual in order to avoid premature excitement.

When he was fragrant and comfortable, he reached for her hand but she stepped back. She was suddenly shy. It was for the man to move on her, but how could she expect it of Stuart, who had only limited use of his limbs? She decided that it had been a long day and she had expended a great deal of energy on pushing the wheelchair. She slipped out, climbed the stair to her own room and went for a long, slow shower, using the sensually perfumed gel that George Tullos had once given her in a fleeting moment of lust. When she was dry, she wrapped herself in a large towel, removed her shower cap and shook out her long curls, brushing them into their natural waves.

Now she hesitated. Was it too soon? If not, what should she wear? Would he expect her to be glamorous, in silk and lace? She had some scandalously appropriate lingerie, gifts from a past admirer at the peak of his unsuccessful pursuit and seldom if ever worn, but was it too early in their relationship for such overt provocation? That admirer had not thought to accompany his gift with a matching negligee. Her old woolly dressing gown was hardly glamorous, but would seem suitably chaste when she had to return through the hall and up the stairs. Life, she decided, was an obstacle course of decisions.

There was a sound from downstairs, of the front door closing.

This, she thought, would be a bad time for her parents to make their return. If they had returned already, some tact and discretion would be called for. There was a creaking on the stairs. She made up her mind. There would be no cowardly evasions. She was a big girl now, too big to allow her life to be restricted by parental expectations. She and Stuart were about to embark on a long-term commitment and the facts had better be faced, the sooner the better. She jerked open the door and stepped out onto the landing.

Councillor Allnith was outside her door. Grace realised too late that she should have followed the Inspector to lock the front door behind him.

This, she decided, might be a good moment for her parents to make a return.

22

Allnith was a different man from the smooth councillor who had spoken to her at the hotel. His clothes were badly matched and looked as though they had been chosen and donned in haste. His gait seemed badly co-ordinated and she could smell whisky on him. His face, twisted in anger, had aged and coarsened. Even his complexion had mottled under the fury that was possessing him – she thought wildly that the evil inside him must be causing him to break out in spots. A flicker of light drew her eye and she saw that he was holding a kitchen knife beside his right thigh. His hand was shaking. The knife looked very new and sharp.

'You bugger,' he said thickly. 'You've sunk me good and proper.'

'Not me,' Grace said. Her voice had gone up to a squeak. She dragged it down again and cleared her throat. 'You were already sunk before I ever heard of you.'

'Balls! I could have had time to clear out. I could have been away and rich if you hadn't started stirring things. I had it planned to perfection.'

Grace kept her head. It would not have been a good time to point out that he had accelerated his own downfall by sending his minions to the attack. 'You still have time,' she said. She tried to inject real urgency into her voice. 'If you hurry, you could be anywhere by morning, but if you use that thing on me they'll extradite you from anywhere on earth.'

He shook his head angrily. 'They're watching my car, I saw them, and they'll have roadblocks at Evelix and

Cambusavie by now. I've no avenue left. I tried the airs-trip but the planes are under guard.' There was spittle running down his chin. He wiped it away with the back of his hand, coming dangerously close to cutting his own throat. 'Your bloody boyfriend has gathered enough evidence to put me away for years and I'm not going to cough any of the money up without a struggle, I'd rather do some extra time and have it waiting for me. So carving you both up won't add more than minutes to my real time and it may give me something to cheer me up, thinking about it while I'm inside. Campbell was ready to take a telling and leave it there, but not you. Oh no! You had to be clever. And now look what your cleverness has brought down on you and your bloody lover. Do you still feel just as clever? Do you?'

If Stuart had cracked the other man's banking codes he could probably track the money to wherever it was tucked away, but if that fact ever dawned on Allnith it would provide him with a motive to kill Stuart outright.

The man was almost beyond reason but Grace's mind went on working with the speed of desperation.

Retreat into her bedroom would be to enter a trap and there was no key in the door. The landing was a puddle of light in a darkened house, square like a fighting ring, but there were exits. Grace began to sidle round the landing. He followed, his right hand pointing the knife like a sword. 'Which is Campbell's room?' he demanded. Grace saw that, in his fury, he had bitten his lip and there was blood mixing with the spittle on his chin.

'He isn't to blame,' she said desperately. 'You said that yourself.'

'If it makes you feel worse, that'll be enough to make me feel better.'

The exchange, though ominous, had won her a moment for thought. She turned and pointed to the door of the linen cupboard, making the turn an excuse for a movement that turned into a dart to his left and towards the head of the stairs. He made a slash at her but he was wrong-footed and she had caught a moment when he was looking away. The swipe was short. Even so, she heard the blade sing as it passed by her ear. Her bare feet gave her a good grip on the carpet. She flew down the stairs four or five at a time. These were the stairs down which she had bounced and thundered as a child and a teenager and the pitch was familiar. She bounced off the wall at the half-landing, took the lower flight in three great leaps and landed in the hall, sliding on a loose rug and almost falling. Behind her she could hear the sound of his feet pounding down but, lacking the confidence born of familiarity, he was slower.

The front door was standing wide open, letting in the cool night air. She had no time for thought, just an instinctive recognition that her momentum was carrying her past it and a refusal to appear in the quiet and respectable street wearing only a bath towel. Nor could she abandon Stuart, for his sake and because of a vague feeling that, even in his enfeebled condition, he would be better than no support at all. Yet, perversely, her instinct was also to lead the maniac away from him.

Her slither on the loose rug had brought her to the dining room door. She aimed one quick scream at the open front door as she turned the handle and threw herself into the dining room, slamming the door behind her. Disastrously, there was no key on the inside of this door either.

She was losing the few seconds grace that she had gained by her precipitous descent of the stairs. She could hear his feet in the hall. Quickly, she retreated round the dining table, already laid in readiness for a family breakfast, and waited, panting. The fire irons that she remembered from her childhood were no longer there and the open fire had been replaced by another electric fake. No poker, then, to brain him with and the table knives had rounded tips. The chairs were too heavy to brandish as weapons.

He entered the room like a rampant bull. She half expected to see steam from his nostrils. Whichever way he came after her, she would be able to dodge round the further side of the table.

But he was beyond logic or care for property. He threw himself onto the table and knelt there for an instant, glaring. Mrs Gillespie's china went flying. Grace was trapped behind the table. He could reach her wherever she ran.

She dived under the table and waited again. Her heart was pounding, her breath refused to come and her mouth was as dry as sandpaper. The stress was mounting until she thought that she would set into a rock and yet a part of her mind could still think. If he had any ability to reason left in his tortured brain, he would surely be watching the direction of the door and, when he tired of the waiting game, that would be the side from which he would come at her. She could hear him moving on the tabletop. She made ready like a sprinter.

The tension broke with a suddenness that, although she was expecting it, made her gag. He hit the floor in a crouch, knife at the ready, about to scramble after her. But she had prepared herself and the tension had made her muscles taut as springs, ready to match his jump with a leap into action. At the first sound of a quick movement above her, she sprang. She was out and up before he could reach her and she dived over the table, rolling as she went and sending more silver and china to the floor. She thought that she had lost her towel but she clasped it round her again.

She hurled herself across the room and out into the hall. She had regained a second or two. Stuart's door was in front of her. His room held some heavy and familiar equipment, which could be used as weapons. If they both had to die they had better die together.

She threw herself at Stuart's door, burst in and turned to slam it behind her. She had a momentary glimpse of Stuart standing naked by the bed, alerted by the sounds of battle. Something obstructed the door's closing and she hurled herself against it, bruising her shoulder, just as a heavy weight thumped and scrabbled at the other side. The latch clicked. Rather than try to use her weight against the door, she gripped the handle and struggled against his attempts to turn it.

How long the remote wrestling continued she never knew. It seemed that for an eternity she was trying to anticipate his twists of the handle while he changed direction, to and fro at the same time throwing himself against the door again and again. The sounds of his assault on the door came through the panels more clearly than his muffled curses and threats. Stuart, without wasting time on useless questions, hobbled naked to join her but his hands were feeble and there was only room for one pair on the handle. Instead, he turned his back to the door and added his weight to hers. Their skin rubbed hotly together. They could feel the battering on the door, strongly.

When the assault on the door suddenly ended, Grace could only think that Allnith had turned away to fetch a

231

tool to break down the door. She turned her eyes to the window. Could she get Stuart out by that route? There was a bed outside the window, filled with roses. But then she realised that the sounds of another struggle were filtering through from the hall, shouts and blows and stamping of feet. As the worst of the noise died and the cursing receded, there came a gentle, polite knock.

She leaned her forehead against her side of the door and breathed deeply.

'Are you in there, Miss Gillespie?' said Detective Inspector Welles's voice. He sounded equally breathless.

'I'm here,' Grace said. 'We're both here.'

'It's over. We have him. Luckily, we came back with some questions and to post a guard. In the nick of time, it would seem. You are all right?'

'Nobody's hurt,' Grace said.

'Do you need any help?'

With the danger past, Grace was feeling light-headed. The question nearly sent her into fits of giggles. 'We can manage without you,' she said. 'You must have your hands full.'

'You won't be bothered again until we come up for your statement in the morning.'

They thanked him and heard him retreat.

Stuart tottered back to his bed. He opened his mouth but words would not come. They looked at each other, wide eyed, but there was nothing to say.

When Grace tried to open the door, she realised that she should indeed have accepted the Inspector's help. At that moment, the play had changed its mood, from Grand Guignol to Whitehall Farce. The resistance to her closing the door had been a fold of her towel that was caught, jamming it solidly. She turned the handle and pulled. She tugged but the door refused to budge. She threw all her weight into a jerk against it. No doubt the struggle had weakened the fixing screws. The handle came away suddenly in her hand, complete with the spindle. She came close to a fall, leaving the towel behind. She heard the other handle drop on the far side. There was now nothing to pull. That door was going to stay closed until the handle was turned on the inside while somebody pushed hard from the hall.

Grace sighed. She was not going to stand there all night. She let the towel fall away and gathered the shreds of her dignity. 'The ethics of my profession require that I stop treating you now,' she said. His face fell. 'But, of course,' she added, 'nobody can stop a wife treating her husband after she retires from practice.'

'Go on, then. Sweep me off my feet.' They exchanged their private smile.

She joined him in the bed. They lay facing, hugging gently, waiting contentedly for passion to rise of its own accord.

Stuart broke the long silence. 'Did you ever hear the story about the little girl on the way home from a family wedding?' he whispered. 'She asked her father, "Daddy, what is fornication?"'

'No,' Grace said. 'I don't know anybody who tells that sort of story. What did her father say?'

'He started to explain, but then he thought of asking her why she wanted to know. And she said, "I heard Uncle Joe say, 'You've just got to have Champagne for 'n occasion like this.'"'

They chuckled together. The vibration was delicious.

Grace asked, 'What put the word fornication into your mind?'

'Can't think,' Stuart said.

* * *

Perhaps because of the physical constraint, their love-making was particularly sweet and tender. In the after-glow, neither felt like speaking. Grace lay and thought of the future. A stable home and a compatible husband. Perhaps a dog and even children.

The presence of an invalid uncle might prove to be a drawback. She might want his room for a nursery. But stroke patients may not live forever and such a life must surely be a burden.

A physiotherapist learns a trick or two.